There Will Be
Wonderful Surprises

Avrom Karl Surath

Printed in the United States of America
Second Printing: June 2007
Book and Cover Design: Brad Lewter
Printed by: Performance Copying & Printing, Sarasota, Florida
ISBN # 978-0-940376-10-6

To my beloved parents, Bill and Ruth,
and to my beloved wife, Ann

Table of Contents

Foreword

Cesareo Pelaez is an extraordinary teacher. His talent first came to my attention when he taught Psychology at Brandeis University. In over fifty years of working with graduate student teaching assistants I have not met his peer. We, the professors, including Abraham Maslow, did our best to get ideas across to sometimes disinterested students. Cesareo did so with ease. He made ideas come alive. His ability to engage the student's mind in meaningful dialogue was unique. He aroused interest, satisfied it and yet left a lingering sense of mild disquietude requiring further inquiry on their part to satisfy.

This talent to arouse, satify and intrigue defines Cesareo's stage performance, indeed the whole of the Le Grand David show. I've attended twice with my grandchildren. It is apparent that the art of the consummate teacher as show-man pleasures and instructs all age groups.

Meeting with members of the Magic Company off-stage revealed facets of Cesareo's personality that I had not fully appreciated. He is an inspired organizer but even more so a charismatic leader who can raise a group to his high esthetic standards. He has woven a clearly exceptionally diverse group of talented individuals into a family. The force of his personality guarantees that their common goal, the preservation and enrichment of an ancient art form, will long endure.

Ricardo B. Morant
Minnie and Harold L.Fierman
Professor of Psychology, Emeritus
Volen National Center for Complex Systems
and Department of Psychology
Brandeis University

May 23, 2006

Foreword

It is impossible not to be captivated by the show that is performed by Le Grand David and his Spectacular Magic Company. It is similarly not possible to categorise the achievement of all those who have contributed to its success. In the wide sweep of world show business there is nothing to compare with the professionalism and amateurism (in the best and original sense of the word) that cohere with love and dedication in this unique spectacle that is *sui generis* or, to paraphrase Lewis Carroll, its own invention.

This book, written and compiled with the devotion and attention to detail one associates with the show itself, will enable future generations to place into more acute perspective the achievement of its founder and leader, Cesareo Pelaez, and the company attracted towards him by the force and power of his personality and example. More than three decades ago this remarkable man set about turning a dream into reality and in the process transformed the small New England town of Beverly on Boston's North Shore into a magnet not only for family audiences so seldom catered for in theatrical terms, but also for magicians and aficionados of wonder from around the globe.

Cesareo's personal achievement transcends that of the conventional hocus pocus peddler, even that of his initial inspiration David Bamberg, who was known to theatre audiences internationally as Fu Manchu. The Pelaez magic extends beyond trickery, misdirection and a showman's bravado to embrace motivational skills that have been admired by psychologists and educationalists alert to the precedent of Cesareo's own teacher, the legendary Abraham Maslow. It was Shakespeare who wrote, "The play's the thing," and "play" is the operative word with this charismatic Cuban, both in the dramatic and the joyous sense. Here—as so seldom in a magic show—is structure, meaning and dramatic thrust; here also is the window to gaiety and gladness that enables a cast of predominantly fully grown adults led by the loyal and engaging David Bull to rediscover the wonder of childhood in their performances and in so doing communicate that feeling to their audiences.

ix

The result is theatre for both child and adult, a world of butterfly splendour and jelly bean delight, where barbershop singers and beautiful mannequins, pantomime animals and accordion-playing clowns, a sorcerer and his apprentice coexist in a swirl of colour and excitement that tugs at the heart strings, enriches the spirit and convinces the most hardened sceptic that there is such a thing as real magic. It is the nearest I have found to the place Dorothy was hoping to find when she set off down the yellow brick road and it is my devout wish that many years from now when the ultimate history of magic as a performance art is written, the spell that is today cast by Le Grand David and his spectacular retinue will still endure. This affectionate volume will help to make that wish come true.

John Fisher
London, May 2006

Foreword

This book tells the true story of a wonderful magic life and many magic moments enjoyed while conjuring it.

It is difficult to explain magic; it is much better to let go, relax, and watch it happen before your eyes. Then you walk away pleased, fulfilled and surrounded by many intriguing questions and deep mysteries of the senses.

It's also practically impossible to dissect a comprehensive driving force such as this book's main subject, separating him from the many souls that comprise his artistic, day-to-day world. But the author, a veteran troupe performer with first-hand knowledge, has done it, in an astonishing, appealing, and captivating way.

And thus you come upon many multi-dimensional surprises; it's what the book's magic pages are all about.

You see, once upon a time and in a far away land, at the age of ten and with my eyes wide open with admiration, I discovered the spark of this fantastic magic life. It was in pre-revolutionary Cuba and his name was Cesáreo Peláez, then a young secular teacher at my Marist Brothers Catholic school. I have known him ever since, although for a long time, due to our separate, forced departures from the Caribbean island and the unexpected forks in the road ahead, our minds were disconnected, we lived in different spheres and circumstances that we could not control.

Back then, in my school, he was dynamic, knowledgeable, creative, demanding, fair, audacious and brave. He was forever stepping out of the box and we were always in awe of the extraordinary lessons he taught, the tales he told, and the things he did. Many years later, I would discover that everyone from those days still respects him without question and smiles warmly when his name comes up. And if he asks, we do it. To me, that is the ultimate test of long-standing loyalty and affection. And it did not surprise me at all that Cesáreo passed with flying colors, even now when we all comb grey hairs.

On the high and low stages of life, where sometimes reality is more dramatic than scripts, the work of an illusionist consists of making realistic-looking illusions; to convince the viewer that something happened when it really didn't. And that in itself brings into focus and summarizes the spectacular person and the peculiar surroundings discussed here.

You see, by means of an innate, God-given conglomerate of superb talents, Cesáreo has created a masterful impression of being the epitome of stage magic, Fu Manchú style. And that he's done magnanimously well.

But underneath the colorful lights and the smoke and the fantastic costumes, beyond the genial gifts that create, direct, choreograph, select, train, develop, motivate and perform, there is a solid rock foundation of extraordinary human values, well-set mores, thought-generating sentiments and boundless skills. Like the artic iceberg, what is not visible is much greater than the impressive and beautiful physical mass above water.

Does the dear reader know that Cesáreo is a trained psychologist?... One who was personally mentored at Brandeis University by the formidable professor and business motivator Abraham Maslow, of Hierarchy of Human Needs fame? Later, Cesáreo dedicated twenty-five of the best years of his life to a professorship at Salem State College. Before that, as mentioned above, he spent nearly ten years teaching and forming young minds at our Catholic high school in Cuba.

And, not surprisingly, with such traditional professional formation and experiences—the fulfilled dreams of a caring father and mother for their loved son—Cesáreo developed and tested the extraordinary people skills and thought process necessary to build the unique team of committed families and individuals that would make Le Grand David and his own Spectacular Magic Company—LGD—an enormous success story.

. . .

Because an Icarus he was not. He did not fly alone and content near the sun until his wax wings melted. Through the years he brought along, guided, and motivated a terrific group of people from all backgrounds, professions and types. Many of them—whole families, actually—have performed in LGD for decades! This is a crucial element, because in stage magic art, as in any group effort, good teamwork is critical to obtain acclaimed success!

In the theater of events described here, the people became as large and important as the force, and the latter would not have it in any other way.

In fact, Cesáreo has executed this approach the whole duration of the journey. He built team spirit with the young Cuban Marists—many of whom still join this writer and Cesáreo himself in an active alumni brotherhood that spans twelve countries and four decades. And he did it too at Salem State, where his psychology classes were always standing-room only. In fact, he was so good a professor and leader that a number of his students joined him to found the LGD magic company, and are still there, now joined in the cast by their spouses and children.

And he did it with the company's performers, the support staff, and their loyal audiences, molding everyone together into a wonderful, dream-come-true, art-business-career format… a creation that has earned them innumerable awards, is in the *Guinness Book of World Records,* and enjoys worldwide recognition from great sages, magi, and connoisseurs of magic. And better yet, it's loved by full-house audiences that, decade after decade, have placed their seal of approval on the whole magic enterprise.

Dear reader, the chapters that follow these lines will open the curtains, turn the spotlights on, and play stupendous Lecuona music across a fantastic spectacle from another era, another galaxy. Just sit back in your theater box, relax, and enjoy a magnificent interpretation about a unique, magical lifetime.

. . .

The tale is told by a fine storyteller... who lived the story as it happened during three exciting decades. He is Avrom Surath, musician, performer, clown, business manager, and now writer of things magic, in addition to everything else he does so well in the company.

With such great players of many good talents, I assure you that you'll see the whole spectacular beauty of the artic iceberg... illusion, or not... ¡Viva la magia!

Luis Puello
Director
MARISTANET-Santa Clara
Coral Gables, Florida

About the Author

Avrom Surath was born and raised in Midland, Michigan. He entered Brandeis University in Waltham, Massachusetts, as a freshman in 1963. Cesareo Pelaez was a graduate student studying with Abraham Maslow and residence counselor for one of the men's dormitories. Avrom met Cesareo the first day of orientation week at the university president's reception for the freshman class. He had just returned from a summer working and traveling in Israel where a flame for learning and living had been fanned. He found a kindred exuberance in Cesareo.

Over the course of the undergraduate years, Cesareo's buoyant friendship was both stabilizing and inspiring for Avrom and many others. Cesareo helped to open psychological viewpoints and vistas for his students and friends. For many, he was the most extraordinary person they had ever met.

After graduating *cum laude* with honors in history, the author entered graduate school at Brown University. He returned to Brandeis in 1969 to continue his PhD studies in medieval history.

In 1972 he met Cesareo by chance in Boston's theatre district. Cesareo had recently started teaching at Salem Stage College. Avrom found himself in the good company of his old friend and the growing circle of young men and women who recognized Cesareo's genius for teaching the fundamentals of living intelligently. He met his wife, Ann, in this group.

Avrom and Ann are among the original members of *Le Grand David and his own Spectacular Magic Company*. They have hosted practically every member of the magic community mentioned in this book including foreword writer John Fisher and his wife, Sue. Along with the Magic Company, Avrom spent happy moments with Ricardo Morant, who wrote a foreword to this volume, on the occasions when Dr. Morant visited. Cesareo's sister, Elisa, was a guest at Avrom and Ann's home. During her stay, she recommended that Avrom reposition his piano to allow himself the beautiful view from his window while playing.

While writing the book, Avrom met and recorded interviews with several Cuban emigres who remembered Cesareo in Cuba. Practically all of them honored him and his wife by staying at their house when they came to Beverly.

"The inspiration for this book came from Cesareo's lips and heart," Avrom says. "My role, to a large extent, has been the scribe. In the Jewish tradition, this is a sacred position. The scribe must keep his thoughts and heart pure so that he can record significant and important events and ideas without distorting them. He also takes responsibility for missing the mark, wherever that may have occurred.

"My father, whose wisdom and love continue to guide me long after his death, held Cesareo in high esteem. He valued his psychological soundness and generosity. What the father strives for from the depths of his being, the son is bound to attempt to complete."

There Will Be
Wonderful Surprises

Chapter One: Teacher

"There was a young fellow by himself in a corner of the lobby," Cesareo recalled. "Despite my fatigue and jet lag, I called him, 'Come over, come over, better to have company than sit alone.' It occurred to me what needed to be done for his sake at that moment."

The young man came over to Cesareo and told him his name, "Owen." They were sitting in the lobby of Logan Hall at the University of London's Institute of Education, near the famed West End theatre district. Cesareo, exhausted from the transatlantic flight, was experiencing jet lag. Nevertheless he made the effort to engage the young man. Owen was sixteen years old. Cesareo told him a little about his stage magic show and asked why was he in the corner. He answered that the older people are very difficult to talk with. Cesareo responded, "Well I'm talking with you."

They were at the centenary of The Magic Circle, a most respected organization of magic performers, aficionados, collectors and historians. It was a four-day conclave attended by nine hundred Circle members from forty-three countries. Cesareo is an Honorary Member of the Inner Magic Circle with Gold Star (one of only a handful who hold its highest level of membership). A featured event of the four day convention was "Meet the Legends," in which five magic luminaries from the world over would participate in a panel discussion before a large audience. Cesareo had been selected as one of the "legends."

As they talked, Cesareo learned that Owen was adept at card and coin manipulations and that he wanted to be a mathematician. As they were sitting together, one person after another came up to greet Cesareo, so he began to introduce Owen to some of the magicians whose acquaintance would be valuable to him. Owen was beginning to get an idea of who he was sitting with after several of them congratulated Cesareo for having the finest and most unique stage magic show they had ever seen. The young man was very impressed with all this and Cesareo laughed with him about it. Owen began to ask him questions. Cesareo responded that he was not going to answer his questions then, "But the day I am interviewed as the celebrity, I'll talk to you directly and answer the questions from the stage." And that he did.

At the "Meet the Legends" symposium later that week the panelists and moderator were seated in historic hand-carved and richly upholstered chairs that had been the front seats in St. Georges Hall—the second of the two theatres run by the legendary magicians Maskelyne and Devant in the early 1900s in London. The setting was impressive and elegant in its simplicity. In his introductory remarks the moderator noted that Cesareo is the only magician ever to be given an Honorary Doctorate of Fine Arts for his work in magic and theater. Cesareo was joined on stage by gentlemen from Italy, England, Ireland and Australia.

Cesareo describes the scene: "So there it begins and the moderator asked a question, what do you think of magic and so on. He addressed the panelist who was sitting by my side. He talked for a little while. When he finished speaking the moderator turned toward me and asks, do you agree with that, Cesareo? And I say very firmly, no I do not agree. Suddenly everybody got tense. The whole

2

audience turned to look at me. No I do not agree, and I began to explain that there are two worlds of reality, a world outside and a world inside, and that we always talk about the world outside and the things outside and we forget that it's the world inside that is the one that creates that magic outside. I began to talk about the world inside.

"Everybody was sitting in heightened attention. Later on in the day a lot of people came up to me and wanted to hear more about that idea. But the interview continued and the next question that came was 'who are the most influential magicians in your life?'

"All the other panelists are talking about famous magicians and when it was my turn, I was thinking of Owen, who asked me that same question—what are the important magicians you have met in your life and who influenced you? I had told him, look, I will answer when I am on stage.

"So I answered: 'First the most important magicians in my life were my father and my mother. My father taught me what magic was. One year on *el Dia de Reyes Magos* [in many Spanish-speaking nations, Christmas gifts are brought January 6, the Epiphany, by the three wise and magical kings] when I found a guitar that was a present for me, I knew there was magic in the world. And the same with my mother.'

"'The next ones were my teachers who taught me to think logically and psychologically and rightly, so that I could understand the world better.' And after that I could begin to talk about magicians, as everybody else had. I recalled Fu Manchu, Ricciardi the father, Ricciardi Junior, Chang, etc., etc. and et cetera. People began to laugh with my et ceteras and to applaud.

3

"Nobody thought of that answer, that the most significant magicians in your life, I say, are your parents. This is what I was telling Owen. You make your parents magic and they make you magic. Wow!"

Owen was fascinated with all this. After the symposium he was ready to move to America to join the company and to continue his studies in America. Cesareo told him that his family came first. He advised him to complete his schooling in England. As the centenary progressed they talked more. "Each day I raised his age—to seventeen, the next day eighteen—it became a running joke. You're getting older because you are getting more mature in your questions," Cesareo told him.

At the end of the convention Owen brought his mother to Cesareo. She introduced herself. Cesareo told her what a wonderful job she had done with her son, and she thanked him for his friendship with him.

Owen wrote this account of his meeting Cesareo:

> Cesareo was tired on this first morning, and the conversation started off seemingly reluctantly. It was only when I said something that Cesareo disagreed with, that I realised how intently he had been listening . . . From how I spoke of myself, and others, to performance technique, no stone was left unturned (or at least that was how it seemed); not only were these stones turned, they were uplifted. Everything I had considered was altered.
>
> Cesareo always seemed calm, he thought about every question before replying with an often concise, but effective, response, sometimes giving a

4

rhetorical answer, and others the simple, "you have four days to discover that." However, this view was shattered on the second day when Cesareo formed a part of the "Meet The Legends" interview panel. When asked where he thought magic came from, Cesareo passionately related his beliefs. The whole audience sat in awe as this man, always so gentle, became so animated as he recounted his opinion of where magic comes from, the heart, and who gives it to us, our parents. More sides of Cesareo were to bloom later in the celebrations, sometimes the trickster, other times a father figure, always generous with his time, and knowledge. I was introduced to everyone, some people Cesareo insisted that I introduce myself to, forcing me to do what I clearly would not have had the nerve to do without his insistence.

Every conversation and every direction Cesareo gave me was meaningful. Looking back, I feel that I came away from the convention as a more mature person, and also more youthful, in my ability to have fun.

Cesareo recalls, "It was very beautiful. I was happy that perhaps I left him with a possible new perspective on the world. At one moment he wanted me to recommend a book for him. Knowing his interest in science and mathematics, I said, yes I will, but please don't read it until you are 21 years old. Then I wrote in the journal he was keeping, *In Search of the Miraculous* by Peter Demianovich Ouspensky, who was, among other things, a noted scientist and mathematician. I was reminded of something I said to one of the young men in our company when he began peforming a clown role on stage as a teenager: 'One thing I cannot give you, that only comes from forty years of living, is a lightness of being.'"

Owen came to visit Cesareo in Beverly with his parents that fall and saw the show about which he had heard so many wonderful things.

Perhaps this story demonstrates how Cesareo teaches: in the midst of life, by using more or less ordinary events. The teaching is psychological and involves those close to the listener or student; it's both intuitive and imaginative, and it is sufficiently indirect, so that you may not even be aware that learning was occurring. You may not even be aware that he is a teacher.

The eminent literary critic Harold Bloom once commented that while Shakespeare's writings teach us how to talk with ourselves, Cervantes instructs us how to talk to one another. Cesareo reveres the Spanish author, and he is fond of quoting from *Don Quixote*. One of his favorites is "Better bad company than none at all." Cesareo's bent is social. He strives to be engaged with others. This has been his way from his youth in Cuba to Brandeis University, to the foundation of a human growth center in New Hampshire in the late 1960s, and ultimately through his tenure as college professor and the establishment of his stage magic company in Beverly.

As a young man in Cuba he was popular, admired and a natural leader. His deep set eyes blazed forth from beneath black brows. His handsomeness was due in part to his aristocratic Spanish nose inherited from his father, Constantino, who sank his roots in Cuba but wisely never gave up his Spanish citizenship. His eyes and nose have rounded and softened with age. His face is not creased, on the contrary, it retains much of the smoothness and softness of youth.

6

The eyes are quick to welcome you—leading the rest of his face into a heartmelting and disarming smile that communicates genuine happiness. His smile reassures you that everything is all right, there is reason for joy, and the prospects are pleasant. It tells you that even though a curve ball may be on its way to you, you will be able to gauge it well and smother it with your bat. Cesareo not only has a way of putting you at ease; he makes you feel as if the world were a theatre created for your own personal triumph. And with your triumph all creation rejoices. What Ben Johnson said of Shakespeare applies to what it's like to be with Cesareo: "I never felt more myself than when in his company."

His former students—some in public office, teachers, business people, householders—happily come up to him in the lobbies of his Cabot Street Cinema Theatre, on the street, in restaurants and recall to him how his classes changed their lives. One middle-aged woman recently introduced herself to him in the lobby on her way to see a film and told him that she still remembered his lectures on Abraham Maslow's humanistic psychology: "When I find myself in difficulties and need something to pull myself out, I recall what you taught us about self-actualization, and this inspires me to overcome what I am facing. I have silently thanked you many times over the years," she said.

He received an Honorary Doctorate in Fine Arts from the Montserrat College of Art in 2004. During the ceremony, the chairman of the college's board of trustees read the diploma to Cesareo standing by his side:

> An acclaimed illusionist, he understands the importance
> of passing a strong sense of reality on to the next
> generation.

7

A supporter of education, psychology, and the arts, he has been a mentor and friend to those who have been fortunate to come under his tutelage at Salem State College, where he was a valued professor, and at the Cabot Street Cinema Theatre and the Larcom Theatre, where he has performed as Marco the Magi with his troupe more than 2,000 times over three decades. Winner of numerous accolades for his artistry, he also replaced over-commercialization with an insistence on quality. A visionary who found an empty space and saw a magical community appear, he has worked to elevate the value of the arts both locally and nationally and in doing so has made the North Shore a better place to live.

In the initial letter to Cesareo which expressed their wish to honor him, the president of the college wrote that they intended:

> ...to recognize your outstandingly creative career as a magician, your founding and direction of *Le Grand David and his own Spectacular Magic Company,* and the important work you have done to restore and bring to life two antique theaters in our city. For our faculty and students, you have been an inspiring creative force committed to both the traditions of your field and to searching new territory.

At the commencement exercises, a thunderous ovation greeted him as he stood to receive the diploma. As the audience grew quiet in anticipation of his acceptance address, through his tears, he recited only these lines and took his seat:

Aunque el fruto
que dé tu sembrado
no lo llegue tu mano a tomar
Siembra siempre
la vida es sembrar
es sembrar
es crecer
es amar.

The lines are from a poem called "The Country Teacher" by Gabriela Mistral (1889-1957), the first Latin American woman to receive the Nobel prize in literature (1945). They translate as:

Even though you do not get
to see the fruit of your labors
Sow, always sow
life is to sow
is to sow,
is to grow,
is to love.

Mistral became a teacher at the age of sixteen and taught her whole life. Teaching was her calling; she considered it a sacred trust.

Cesareo studied psychotherapy in his native Cuba with one of its leading psychotherapists. She asked him one day what he wanted for himself in life. He answered, "I want to be great."

She told him, "If you wish to be great, then go up to the mountains and teach the poor." He became a teacher at age eighteen. His instructor and mentor, Brother Mauro Lopez, the director of the highly regarded Marist Brothers academy in Santa Clara, Cuba, recognized "gold" and hired him as a lay instructor in 1951 and watched over his development as an educator.

9

Cuba was arguably one of the most advanced Spanish-speaking societies in the world during Cesareo's youth. Its polyrhythmic music was a primary influence on the pioneers of contemporary American jazz and classical music. After a visit to Cuba in 1932 George Gershwin wrote "Rumba," later renamed "Cuban Overture." In an effort to teach Americans about the island's sophisticated rhythms, he illustrated the opening page of the score with the Cuban percussion instruments featured in the piece, and instructed that the various drums and other rhythmic instruments be placed in front of the orchestra next to the conductor.

Cuba was the only Latin American nation where the peso was equal to one dollar. Havana, known as the most exotic city in the Americas, had been a shipping crossroads for centuries, the port at which European trading vessels stopped on their way to and from South and Central American destinations. During Cesareo's childhood, the Astors, the Vanderbilts, the DuPonts, and Will Rogers wintered in Havana. It was the capital of the largest republic in the Caribbean and was growing rich from its robust trade with the United States. Havana's streets were wide, palm-lined boulevards suited to the traffic of its many automobiles; it was incomparably more cosmopolitan than a beach town ninety miles north called Miami. It boasted the most Cadillacs per capita of any city in the world.

With its gorgeous parks and plazas, the enormous baroque headquarters of its Galician and Asturian communities (The *Palacio*

Centro de Gallego housed the National Opera House), a presidential palace decorated by Tiffany & Co., and a capitol building modeled on that of the United States, it was one of the world's most beautiful cities. Desert winds were still blowing tumbleweed across Las Vegas when Havana was attracting a refined international clientele to its lush hotels with casinos and floor shows.

By the 1950s, Havana's famous department store *El Encanto* was among the finest in the world. Its patrons included Errol Flynn, Robert Taylor, John Wayne, Tyrone Power, Ray Milland, Debbie Reynolds, Pier Angelli, Lana Turner, and many other celebrities. Havana's thirty-nine-story FOCSA *(Fomentos de Obras y Construcciones S.A.)*, completed in 1956, was the second tallest concrete building in the world. It housed thirty floors of condominiums and nine floors for multiple use, including a movie theater, toney retail stores, a supermarket and even a television studio. The typical floor had thirteen condominiums: five units with three bedrooms and maid's quarters and eight with two bedrooms and maid's quarters. The three-bedroom apartments sold for 21,500 pesos at a time when the median price for a single-family home in the United States was around $15,000.

Cuba was the first Latin American nation with black and white television (1950), and was the second nation in the world (after the U.S.) to have color television. It was the first Latin American nation to have three color television stations (1957; Miami did not have color TV broadcasting until 1964). Its first railroad began operations in 1837, eleven years before Spain's. It was the first Latin American nation to have a printing press (1723), a public electric lighting system (1889), and electric street cars (1900).

12

In 1920 Enrico Caruso made a concert tour of Cuba, performing at the National Opera House and also at *El Teatro de la Caridad* (Theatre of Charity) in the city of Santa Clara. Cesareo's mother was in the audience and often told him the story of how the crowd overflowed the theatre onto the *Parque Vidal* where Caruso's voice carried cleanly and clearly. It was in the neighborhood of *El Teatro la Caridad* that Cesareo spent his earliest years. The theatre had a large silver screen that "flew" to the rafters to allow for its live stage attractions. Otherwise, movies were shown, usually in two- or three-day engagements. There was never a dark night. As a cinema it featured many American films: "And what movies I saw. By my late teens, all the great Broadway musicals were being made into movies. I used to favor the 5:00 pm showing, called *tanda elegante,* which was the showing attended by the theatre aficionados, including many of the society ladies, who dressed elegantly," Cesareo recalls.

The theatre was built in the late nineteenth century by Santa Clara's most renowned philantropist, Marta Abreu (1845-1909). Santa Clara was known as "the City of Marta" because of her far-sighted beneficence. She built and staffed medical clinics, schools for waifs and underprivileged children, general public schools, and a home for the aged (suppported by ticket revenues from *El Teatro de la Caridad)*. She built bridges and public laundromats. In 1895, she funded the construction of plants to generate electricity and refine natural gas.

El Teatro de la Caridad and the *Parque Vidal* were at the heart of Santa Clara, Cuba's fourth largest city, located at the center of the island. The park's white marble gazebo was a majestic blend of neoclassical Greek columns, capitals, and Parthenon-like roof facades with nineteenth-century Spanish balustrade. Here Cesareo would thrill at performances of Santa Clara's bands and orchestras, here families would stroll happily in the early evening—husbands and wives arm in arm, accompanied by their children and friends. The park was surrounded by grand civic structures, cathedrals and mansions of stone with terracotta-tiled patios rimmed by colonnaded arcades. Santa Clara's population was over 100,000 when Cesareo was born in 1932. It was the capital of the *Las Villas* province and was to be home to *Universidad Central de Las Villas,* one of its largest universities, which opened as Cesareo was graduating from high school.

Santa Clara's street-level storefronts and cafes stood below balconies with iron balustrades wrought with intricate Moorish designs. Everywhere there were pastel masonry exteriors overgrown with flowers and lianas. Residences and commercial buildings were distinguished by their native architectural flourishes, like stained glass panels above windows and doors.

As a child, Cesareo heard from his window the singsong of fruit vendors on the street below. They sang the praise of their wares, so succulent and gorgeous. Over generations the vendors' musical hawking inspired a genre of compositions called *pregones*, or street-hawkers' songs. Set to lilting Afrocuban rhythms, *(El Manisero* became an international hit), they worked their way into the minds and hearts of the island's folk the way catchy ditties often do.

"The memories of the first years of my childhood, regarding theatre, are just being an audience for the little shows my older sister Elisa and her friends put on," Cesareo recalled. "When I was three years old my father left us for six months. As I grew up I learned that he left to visit his mother in Galicia, Spain, and to arrange for his brother and sister to come to Cuba. But I felt only loss and missed him very much.

"I remember as a toddler *El Dia de Reyes Magos* when Elisa and her friends played at staging shows at the house, perhaps with costumes they had received that day. They put on Mother's shoes and hats, draped themselves in shawls, and sang and danced. They sat me to be the audience. About a year later, when I was four, I was part of the audience again when my father began to take me to *El Teatro la Caridad* to see shows. I think many times he used me as an excuse to go see the productions that came to town, especially the magic companies, like Fu Manchu [stage name of David Bamberg]. One of my favorites used to be Chang [stage name of Juan Pablo Jesorum]. He was from Panama and one of the teachers of Fu Manchu, in a way. Once I recall he came to town with his own beautiful tent all to stage his show. What an extraordinary experience!"

Cesareo's father, Constantino, set sail from La Coruña, the chief seaport of Galicia, as a sixteen year old. Folk from this region of Spain are known for their clarity and for their down-to-earth and somewhat wry sense of things. They speak their minds and tend to be sincere. La Coruña is connected to the mainland by an isthmus. A Galician saying is that Vigo works, Pentevedra sleeps, Santiago de Compostela prays, and La Coruña dances and sings. Following the custom of his seafaring folk, Constantino made his first global voyage while still a youth. When the vessel docked in Havana, he decided to stay.

"He began working on a coffee plantation and learned everything about the beans," Cesareo recalls. "Then he began to take *muestras* (samples) on the road to sell. He became a coffee broker. Soon he was driving all over Cuba selling 50-pound sacks of coffee beans. He sold thousands of them, he knew the beans so well. During the summers, when I was on vacation from school, he took me with him. I got to know the entire island. When he stopped to call on businessmen and cafe owners, I played outside the car. I had my wonderful fantasies, and I sang and danced around the car. When we drove together, very often we did not speak. I loved to look out the windows at the land, the palms, and at the sand." The Cuban countryside has over ninety varieties of native palm trees. Towering over them all are royal palms and ceiba trees that grow to heights of one hundred fifty feet, flowering trees, and shoreline mangroves obscured by dense forest with leafy trees supporting delicate orchid epiphytes, magnificent flowers whose roots dangle freely from a tree's limbs and derive their sustenance from the atmosphere.

"Eventually my father opened an office in Havana, at the bureau of commerce, where he bought and sold coffee and exported it. He had many sidelines, including importing razor blades, and 'Duro-Block'—a factory that manufactured concrete blocks with machinery he had purchased in the United States that put him in a class with no competitors. He had tremendous public relations skills. Most of his businesses required no inventory. He was a broker, a middleman, the one with contacts and connections.

"He came to own two cafes in Santa Clara's best hotels. Soon commuting to Havana got to be too much. When he decided to move his office back to Santa Clara, he sold all of his beautiful office furniture, except a polished mahogany desk. He brought that back to the house for me. It had a roll top that opened up to drawers. The first time I opened it, what did I find? A new typewriter. My very own typewriter. And you know what else? A real telephone. We had one of the first telephones in Cuba. It's called a candlestick phone because it stood vertically and held the earpiece in a cradle on the side. You spoke into the top of the candlestick and held the other part to your ear. This was in the 1940s. The number was 2234. I remember it now that I am recalling all of this. I had the telephone, but there was no one to call. The calls coming in were for Father."

Having left school after third grade, Constantino was self-educated and self-made. He was among the wealthiest men in Santa Clara and welcome in its most distinguished social circles. He brought his sister Estrella and brother Celso from Spain and settled them in Santa Clara, where they both married and raised their own families. Constantino had married Santa Clara's most beautiful young lady, Genoveva, a winner of the city's beauty contest. He made sure that his children did not get big heads because of the family's social position and was a generous man who enjoyed providing for others. Their house was always full of fruit and delicacies for guests.

Throughout his youth, Cesareo's mother was his primary artistic influence. She hosted *tertulias*—literary and performance gatherings—with artists and musicians who were appearing in the area. Known to all by his nickname "Mirre," probably coined by his father, Cesareo began to rub shoulders with performing artists at an early age. In those years Havana was a port of call for some of the world's greatest entertainers. They were attracted not only by the beauty of the island, but also by its lively culture. This was reflected in glorious buildings dedicated to theatre and the arts. Cuba's colonial architecture, like that of the United States, had its own simple charm. But, beginning in the late nineteenth century, its newly constructed theatres and civic buildings blended European neoclassical, baroque, and Moorish grandeur with native color and delicacy. Cuba's stages featured opera, zarzuela, theatre and magic companies traveling between Europe and South America. One of his friends from that time recalled, "Mirre attended all the touring musical reviews—called *teatro bufo*—that passed through Santa Clara, especially those of Arredondo and Castany and danced in his seat. Sometimes his feet got so carried away that they danced in the aisle."

Constantino and Genoveva's first child was Elisa (named after Constantino's mother), who was four years old when Cesareo was born. Already studying piano, she would go on to become a conservatory graduate and concert performer. Practically every Cuban home, even among the poor, had a piano. It was the tradition for girls to begin studying at an early age and to continue through their teens. Elisa and her friends also studied ballet three times a week, and they all learned English either in school or through tutors.

"Imagine growing up hearing that beautiful music she was playing for hours every day of my childhood," Cesareo commented. Elisa played a complete classical repertoire, from Bach to Albeniz and including the recently published compositions of Granados. Cuban musicians are traditionally grounded in the classics before embarking on the island's magnificent body of popular music, including the danzon, guaracha, rumba, conga, and boleros. In what other land in the world did love songs and infectious dance music blossom forth as they did in Cuba? Many of its native composers, like Ignacio Cervantes, Jose White, Eduardo Sanchez de Fuentes, Jorge Ankermann, Moises Simon, Gonzalo Roig and Ernesto Lecuona, established themselves as concert artists in Europe before returning to their homeland to write, perform and record. Cesareo was immersed in musical luxuriance.

"What an influence! No wonder I learned to sing many of the songs in her repertoire." Cesareo recalled. Eventually he developed into a magnificent tenor. She often accompanied him in concert as they performed in Santa Clara and went on to win national competitions.

Cesareo continued, "When the theatrical companies came to *El Teatro la Caridad,* I saw all the trucks and props and apparatuses being delivered to the side of the theatre. Chang had painted the boxes that contained his illusions with a big portrait of his head and hands making a prestidigitator's gesture. I used to like to watch those things and was very impressed by the boxes and the unloading of the scenery. That impressed me as much as the performance itself.

"My first grade teacher used to teach us to read by bringing a huge, enormous book that he put on an easel. And the book had hand-painted stories, very famous stories. I remember one of the ones that impressed me was the 'Tower of Babel.' From the easel he taught us the letters and reading. We began to use scissors to cut out letters. It was a different kind of teaching; it was a different kind of school; we had Thursdays off instead of Saturdays, so the week went from Monday to Wednesday, Thursday off, and then Friday and Saturday, and Sunday off. So, Thursday I knew was a day my father would take me to the theatre.

By the third or fourth year of elementary school, Cesareo formed his first theatre company using a pair of scissors. He cut figures from old magazines after his aunt, mother, and sister had finished with them. The cutout figures became the actors. The company traveled from one venue to the next in toy trucks he had received as holiday gifts. He cut out letters to make advertisements for the show which he glued to the sides of the trucks. Lined up in a caravan, his circuit began in the kitchen. The show traveled through all the rooms of his home, all the way to the living room, while stopping in each room for a performance. Then the whole company went back to the storage room until the next trip.

"January 6, called *El Dia de los Reyes Magos,* is when our Christmas presents used to come," Cesareo recalled. "They were brought by the three wise men, the magi, and they put them under your bed. On this holiday during one of my elementary school years, I reached under the bed and I heard a noise—a beautiful hum of chords. This is the year that I got a guitar. I was eight or nine. I was so happy with my guitar. It was very high quality for an eight year old. My mother arranged for me to study guitar at the conservatory that Elisa attended.

"My teacher was a black gentleman trained in classical and popular music; he was the guitar teacher in the conservatory. The first thing he taught me about the guitar was that it was alive and therefore to treat it with all the love and thoughtfulness I would give to my beloved. He taught me to cherish it in the way I touched it and held it. The first song he taught me was *La Habanera Tu*, a very beautiful piece, which ends with the lyric *porque Cuba eres tu* (because you are Cuba). He was a wonderful musician and insisted on the correct rhythm. I learned so much from him and played *La Habanera Tu* a lot. If I put a guitar in my hands now, I could play it, after so many years. Those are the tricks of the unconscious."

Cuba has a rich musical history that brought African, French, English and Spanish influences into a unique mix beginning in the eighteenth century, or earlier. By 1800 a sizable black population had purchased its freedom from slavery. Both blacks and whites were trained in schools of music that were established along the European classical tradition. In the nineteenth century, Cuban composers infused the popular English contradance, brought to the island by traders and colonialists, with rumba and congo rhythms as they composed and published their *danzas* and *danzones*. The island's music has been racially mixed for centuries. It is a blend, known as *mestijaze*—like a rope whose strands have become more inextricably bound as the centuries passed.

Havana's *Teatro Principal*, where Cuban audiences viewed European classical works, was inaugurated on October 12, 1776. Theatrical life developed throughout the island, and soon *teatro bufo*, or farcical theater, began to appear. It humorously characterized and lampooned the different ethnic groups in Cuban society. Around this time there began to appear popular musical reviews called *tonadillas* and one-act light operettas called *sainetes*. In these shows, guitars, *guiros* (a typical Cuban percussion instrument made from a serrated gourd and stick), and the *tres* (a native three-stringed guitar) accompanied love songs and choral works on stage. Racial distinctions were blurred in these stage ensembles. Like stand-up comics of today their satires parodied every element of society.

Bufo theatre had a stock of standard characters. There was the streetwise trickster *(el negrito)* always outsmarting the *gallego*, the first generation Spanish immigrant. The *gallego* was very hard working, typically a café owner, saved his money—he was a penny-pincher—and was very responsible. Sometimes *el gallego* represented the colonial bosses and politicians. One way or another, *el negrito* tricked him into doing something he needed done. Then there was *la mulatta* (sometimes known as *la rumbera*), an astonishingly beautiful, saucy woman who loved to dance and sing, and with whom all the

21

were in love. Other characters included *guajiros* (peasants), hunters, Chinese laundrymen, timbales and bongo players, carriage drivers, and *ñañigos* (spiritualists and healers). Cuba was always a melting pot, and the humor with which late nineteenth-century American vaudeville skewered its new citizens, recently arrived immigrants, and old power brokers was commonplace in Cuba by 1812. Typically, white actors applied blackface in *bufo* companies. Often the comedy was set in the *solara,* the courtyard which the apartments of a tenement building faced. Here *el gallego, el negrito, la mulatta* and the others, who all lived in the tenement, played out their dramas. No matter how complicated and thick the plot, things would always come to a proper, happy resolution, one way or another. At the end, everyone danced. It was on stage that social tensions relaxed into a happy unity.

Cesareo embraced the "bothness" of Cuban culture: the African and European, the native and the colonial, the classical and the vernacular. Constantino was Spanish and never gave up his Spanish citizenship. Genoveva was Cuban. Father fostered a distrust of the clergy and the hierarchical nature of the Church. Mother moved in a very Cuban circle that believed in mediums, in trance states and possession, in spiritualism, in psychic phenomena and the like. Cesareo also witnessed Santeria and other native African religions brought to the island—some dressed as Christianity in order to survive—in which black priests and dancers subsumed the healing powers of their gods around bonfires with bongos pulsing inspiring rythyms, the ground strewn with small, smooth black stones, chicken and fish bones, red rooster feathers, and magical turtle and snail shells perfumed with *agua de rosas.* Constantino insisted that Cesareo receive the very best education, which meant training by Marist brothers in a private

22

Catholic school. His son was encouraged by these circumstances to come up with his own *mestijaze*—a fervent faith expressed in his own idiom.

The highlight of Cesareo's pre-teen years was learning to play guitar and sing, which was a happy consolation once asthma began to prevent him from playing baseball, in particular from running the bases and playing outfield. During that time, when he could not sleep due to the asthma, he read Nobel prize winners in literature.

"As I was passing from elementary school to high school *(bachillerato)* I began to get together with other young fellows, some were older and better guitarists, and at every opportunity we went serenading. We developed a repertoire because we began close to midnight and serenaded until sunrise, ending up at one of the members' home for breakfast. We did it for Mother's Day, birthdays, really any opportunity we got. This custom of all-night festivities was called *noche de ronda.*

"All this eventually disappeared because of politics. The politics began from very early to get involved in every aspect of life. I remember the first time I realized this was just after learning to read. My very best friend Manolo—we might have been seven or eight years old—lived just a block away. I used to go to his house, he used to come to my house. We sat next to each other every day on the school bus. One day he was not there, the seat was empty. There was no one in his house, they all disappeared. That was the first loss of any signifance for me and I was told that it was because his parents were in a 'political thing.' Nobody ever told me what happened. I only felt his disappearance and he never came back."

The serenades stopped because Batista established curfews for political reasons. People could not be on the streets after a certain hour. It became too dangerous for serenades and parties. Eventually, after Cesareo left the island, he stopped playing the guitar forever.

"I was not into politics. We liked to have parties, we enjoyed fun and high spirits. I remember so well a New Year's Eve celebration when my father began to dance *la jota*. He was such a good dancer. Then, for a party for his business, he hired a dance company to dance *la jota* with him. I was fascinated with this and became an incredible dancer."

Cesareo's godmother sponsored him in a competition in which he sang and danced and Elisa played the piano. They won first prize. Especially for the contest, his aunt Aurora made him a beautiful costume, which included purple painted boots. He sang a comic folk song about a lady who offers a priest fifty *duros* for his habit. The priest responds, "I'm very sorry, lady, I won't sell it unless I go along with it." At this point, Cesareo broke into a playful rythmic dance. Brother and sister ended performing for charities and fundraising events.

Cesareo performed magic as a child and young man. He taught himself English in order to read the instructions that came with the first illusion he purchased.

He tells, "You know, I always had a handkerchief in my pocket in Cuba. Everyone did. It was a tropical climate and you used it often to wipe your brow. The ones Mother gave me were beautiful white linen monogrammed with 'CP.'"

"As a child of ten or eleven, I think it was around 1942, I loved to

24

perform a little trick. I used to take my handkerchief from my pocket and open it on the palm of my hand. I took a wooden toothpick from another pocket and placed it in it. Then I carefully folded the kerchief over the toothpick, and held the wrapped toothpick vertically in my hand. I asked one of the gentlemen watching to break the toothpick, which he promptly did. Then I asked if he would break it again. Snap. Again. Snap."

"I unfolded the handkerchief and there was the toothpick—whole and unbroken. I knew that the most important thing was the acting. I performed it graciously, slowly enfolding the pick, gently extending my hand, and with a big smile asking the person to break it. Adults were more surprised by the effect than children.""

As Cesareo approached his teens, Constantino purchased a mansion with an enormous living room and many other rooms that surrounded a large terracotta patio. A wrought iron fence surrounded the property, with "Villa Elisa" (named after Constantino's mother, Elisa) forged above its ornate gates. The perfumes of roses, carnations, lemon trees, crysanthemum, and honeysuckle filled the house. It had a beautiful veranda, garlanded with flowering vines and bougainvillea, and on it was a table custom-built for dominoes. There were three sets of dominoes, all of hand-carved ivory. The foyers had walls and floors of the finest Spanish tile with Moorish designs in rich blues and reds. Its ceilings were very high and the rooms were immense. The veranda opened to a large formal living room with a grand piano. There were four bedrooms: the parents', Elisa's, Aunt Aurora's, and Cesareo's. Beyond the living room was a family room that opened onto a courtyard surrounding the patio. Facing the patio from the other direction was the dining room, off of which was the kitchen. Behind the villa and attached to it was a four-car garage.

"Sometimes I would play the teacher with my friends on our veranda. I arranged the chairs and benches into a classroom and would pretend I was teaching the class.

"We were the first in the neighborhood to get a television. In the evenings, everyone came over to watch. Sometimes there would be a couple of hundred people, and they were all welcome.

"We had two mango trees that bore hundreds of fruits. One tree was female. Its fruit was so succulent that all you had to do was puncture it and you could squeeze it and drink its nectar right from the fruit. The male was tougher. That one you had to peel and slice if you wanted to eat it.

"Mother raised lots of doves and had a *palomar* (dove house) for them. All day you could hear the birds sing—not only the doves, but also cuckoos, finches, wrens, and warblers. In our back yard we kept hens and two magnificent peacocks. Mother fed the birds and fowl every morning.

"Lobolo was our rotweiler. She had such beautiful eyes. Every year she had a litter of six or seven pups. We gave them away, and we had a waiting list. So many years later, I remember her so well."

Don Constantino Pelaez -
Cesareo's father.

Mirre at 7 years old.

Mirre and his mother,
Dona Genoveva Perez de Pelaez.

Teatro la Caridad, Santa Clara, Cuba.

Parque Vidal, Santa Clara, Cuba.

Teatro la Caridad, Santa Clara, Cuba.

Chapter Three: Mirre's Follies

It was not until high school that Cesareo began to put together a theatrical company with a group of friends. It came to be known as "Mirre's Follies" and numbered close to two dozen members. The first two girls were Elisa's students. Elisa by now was teaching music and these two girls learned what Cesareo was doing and wanted to join. One of them, Gloria Sanchez (now married and living in Miami Beach), was twelve. She was among several members of Mirre's Follies who rediscovered Cesareo fifty years later. As Cesareo gained national acclaim for Marco the Magi's production of *Le Grand David and his own Spectacular Magic Company,* several alumni of Mirre's Follies and of the Marista academy where he taught in Santa Clara flew to Beverly to visit him. Gloria recalled, "We started in the garage of Mirre's house. We made the curtains and hung them. We rehearsed at his home, often in the patio around which the house was built. It was a large home, and it was always full of young people. There would be someone practicing in a room over here; Aunt Aurora, who made our costumes, was in another part of house; there was a big patio in the middle where we all got together and everybody was happy. Beba, Cesareo's mother, would always be talking—she was very funny, always ebullient. Sometimes you would see her on the porch in her rocking chair listening to the radio. In the 1940s we used to listen to programs like "Classics of the Air," a serial on which great novels would be read. The house belonged to all of us.

"After rehearsals in the afternoon, sometimes Mirre would ask Aunt Aurora to make him steak and *chicharritos,* which were hand-made potato chips. Other afternoons she made us all *duro frio,* ice-cream cubes. This was a real treat, because you could only get these in restaurants and cafes. But Constantino's house had a refrigerator/ freezer (everyone else had ice boxes, if that) that made it possible."

Rene Perez, Cesareo's friend since second grade, recalled that the company was formed in the mid 1940s and lasted through their high school years. Rene describes the type of show they did as *teatro bufo,* "Mirre was extraordinary performing *el negrito.*"

Cesareo remembers, "There were half a dozen professional companies that continually toured Cuba presenting these shows, and I never missed a one."

Rene: "Some of them, like *Pototo y Filomeno,* who played on stage in Havana, were also on the radio. They were famous, fabulously successful, and were influential in Cuban arts and culture. The first part of our show, which took about an hour, was this traditional *bufo* comic scenario. Mirre wrote all of the episodes. They were mainly satire, poking fun at politics or various social situations. The first part ended with all the company joining in a typical Cuban dance."

Their friend Manolito played *el gallego,* and the beautiful Violeta, another neighborhood friend, played *la mulatta.* After a fifteen-minute intermission, Cesareo took the role of master of ceremonies for the second part of the show, called *Variedades.* He introduced the numbers, and sometimes sang arias from popular zarzuelas, his operatic tenor charging skyward, a vocal Pegasus.

Variedades featured typical Cuban dances, such as the *chancleta* (the dancers wear wooden sandals also called *chancleta*—the dance has similarities to American tap and Flamenco), rumbas (Violeta was *la rumbera*, Cesareo *el rumbero*), and Spanish dances such as *el jota*. Rene danced a tango with his partner and usually sang ("I performed whatever song Elisa selected for me"), and there were a number of other singers who appeared, some of whom went on to become popular entertainers in Cuba. One of them, Doris, who had a beautiful mellow voice, was nicknamed "Mani." *El Manisero* was the highlight of her repertoire.

The second part also included traditional circus and vaudeville capers, and other dollops of light and happy entertainment. For example, Cesareo was an exceptional impressionist. In one of his numbers, he spoofed the manner of Spanish spoken by people from different parts of Spain, Cuba, and South America. His comic mastery of accent, inflection, vocabulary, gesture, facial expression, and movement kept his audiences in stitches. He also performed hilarious impressions of dance couples from France, England, Spain, and Cuba with an imaginary partner and a set that consisted of two chairs only.

El negrito was also a trickster, and often had a magical prank up his sleeve. This character may have introduced stage conjuring to *bufo* theatre audiences as early as the eighteenth century in Cuba. It was in the *Variedades* part of his show that Mirre performed classic magic routines. One was a comic mentalist number with his friend Manolito and one of the girls in the company. On a vertical board were the numbers zero through nine. Manolito, the "mind-reader," was blindfolded on the other side of the stage. The girl would point to a number, say, three, for example. Cesareo would walk to Manolito and ask him if he could identify which number she had selected, very visibly tapping him three times on the shoulder. Manolito would say three and the audience began to laugh. Then the girl picked seven, and Mirre repeated the procedure with Manolito, this time tapping seven times. Finally, the girl picked zero. Mirre comically mimed the zero in different ways while he made his compulsory walk to Manolito. As he asked the blindfolded "seer" which number she had picked, he smacked him on his rear, Manolito immediately blurted out, "Zero!"and the audience roared.

Mirre also performed the classic Egg Bag illusion with Manolito. He placed an egg into a cloth bag, then showed the bag empty and then immediately produced a live chicken from the bag. "It was our chicken. We kept chickens, peacocks, and white doves at the house," Cesareo said.

Violeta recalls, "We began by building a theatre in Mirre's father's garage. It was a very large four-car garage. His father removed two of the cars so that we could use the rest of the space. I helped to paint the proscenium that was built out of cardboard and paper-mache. Mirre was everywhere, telling this one this, and that one that, directing something else over there, and everything had to be perfect. He was a perfectionist. Once he said to me, 'No, no, that's wrong!' and I started to cry. Then Elisa came over to me and said, 'Violeta, you don't have to listen to him. It's all right. Just keep going.'

"I was *la rumbera*," she recalls. "I danced the rumba with *el negrito rumbero*, Mirre's character. His Aunt Aurora made me a beautiful *rumbera's* dress, with row upon row of ruffles in the skirt. You knew that Mirre was born for the theatre from the way he directed. He taught me how to dance for the stage, and performing with him and with the company was exhilarating. It was ultimately a very sane theatre company, very decent and disciplined. And we had fun.

"Practically every afternoon at 4:00 Aunt Aurora would make *duro frio* for Mirre and those of us who were rehearsing would join him for the frozen chocolate treat. Some afternoons we would go to one of his father's cafes for Cuban coffee and *flan* (caramel custard). These were the happiest days of my life. My family left Cuba for the United States in early 1959. We brought nothing with us, because we thought we would be returning in a matter of weeks or a few months. So, from those days with Mirre's company, I have not even a single photograph. But I have the happiest memories and a gratitude and affection that will never die."

Rene: "Mirre was very intense performing his characters and he was a big hit. That's what made the show so popular, I think. He was very dedicated, he was an extraordinary person, really. He was at the top of his class, very bright, and completely passionate about his work as an artist. As a director, he was of impeccable character. He liked to have things well organized and for people to show up on time for the rehearsals, and was very attentive to everyone. But, don't cross his path or disobey his direction, or he will not mince his words. Once we were rehearsing for a show in *el Teatro la Caridad*, and things were not proceeding as they should. Right then and there he screamed, 'Nobody's paying attention. That's it, there is no show.'

"Boom, he jumped off the stage, and left. Everyone ran after him, begging, 'Mirre, you have to think it over, no you cannot do it.'

"Mirre retorted, 'No, I am tired of all this.' But after a while, he would calm down and return to continue the rehearsal for the next show. Elisa was a gifted pianist. She was really unbelievable. And not only classical music, which she performed magnificently and often in public concert. She also played Cuban dances and boleros.

31

And she gave our theatre company her all.

"We would say, 'I want to sing such and such a song in the *Variedades* part of the show,' and she would transpose it to our voice range and accompany us. Like Mirre, she had no hair on her tongue. If we did not follow her instructions, we heard, 'You know what, I'm not going to play for you. You are not following directions, and here we have been rehearsing for three hours for nothing.' She and her brother were a team, partners. It was really amazing, and let me tell you, we had wonderful memories, and those years were the best. Because everything was done voluntarily, because we wanted to do the work and we all loved what we were doing.

Cesareo: "We were such good friends and some of us had been together so long that we developed our own language. For example, we had a word that only we understood—*pukiti*—that we used to alert one another when we thought someone was trying to pull the wool over our eyes or were pretending to be something they weren't."

Rene: "We charged twenty-five cents admission to the shows in Mirre's garage. Then we began performing in his home. Many of the rooms faced the patio, and we used the dining room as the stage. We would push Elisa's piano all the way back onto the side of the stage, down where the orchestra pit would be. We built curtains and sets for the stage, and my cousin Domingo, who is now an architect and engineer in Chicago, was in charge of lighting and special effects. We nicknamed him *El Luciérnaga* (the firefly). The public sat in the patio. It was really a full-fledged mini-theatre."

Domingo: "We made our own paint for the backdrops. We used organic glue with no chemical additives and heated it. We purchased the color as a powder from the paint company. Then we mixed the powdered colors with the hot glue to make the paint. I remember making the most beautiful orange for one of our backdrops."

Cesareo recalls, "Actually we started on top of a chicken coop *(el gallinero)*. We used the roof of the coop for our stage at first. When we moved to the garage, we used Mother's bed sheets as curtains. We laced them, and I cut beautiful hearts in red and pasted them all over the curtain, and *voilà,* we had a red hearts curtain. We used the money we made from admissions to go to see shows downtown. We sat in the cheap seats in the top galleries. Although at the time I thought the ticket price was steep, it really wasn't. But we paid our own way, and that was a big thing for us."

Pedro, Rene's brother was a talented percussionist and had found his place next to the piano, accompanying Elisa. Over time they outgrew the patio; their next stage was a large warehouse in Santa Clara. After the warehouse, the company performed in the social hall of one of the largest Catholic Churches in Santa Clara, The Church of the *Buen Viaje.* There was a full stage, large backstage and wings, dressing rooms, and extensive lighting resources.

Gloria recalls, "Mirre taught me how to perform on stage, how to sing, how to carry my body in dance, how to move, what to do with my hands, choreography, everything. He literally taught me how to sing and how to dance. These were the happiest days of my life. I flew to rehearsals, which were required. You did not miss one for any reason, and I loved them. Eventually we performed at *Teatro de la Caridad,* which was an honor, since it was such a great theatre.

"During the twelve days of Christmas *(las posadas)* we went house to house, singing *Villansicos* (carols). The families put their name and address on paper if they wanted us. The tradition was to create

33

beautiful nativity scenes in each house or yard. The neighborhoods gave out awards for the best. It was by these creches that we gathered to sing. They served us *pastellitos* and coke. Cesareo taught us how to sing the carols.

Cesareo: "Everyone in the neighborhood created beautiful nativity scenes at their homes. I used to build one each year and worked without rest until it was finished. My nativity scene covered the entire living room. It was absolutely immense. In some homes the tradition was to build everything to have it ready for the three magical wise kings, whose figures were placed in the setting only on the eve of *El Dia de Reyes Magos.* I used to place the kings from the first day of Christmas very far away from the manger in three diffeent parts of the room. Then each day I would move them a little closer, until the eve of the Epiphany, when they would come together."

Rene: "The creativity of those days was amazing. There was no money to spend on costumes, scenery, and so forth. So, everyone used to go out and look for whatever was needed. My mother had about four or five aunts, and they were very active socially in Camajuani, a town about 45 minutes from Santa Clara, on the road on which Mirre lived, the *Carratera de Camajuani.* We traveled there and asked them, 'Well, all the gowns you have from dances that you don't plan to use, we need them.' They put them all in a suitcase and brought them so that they would be made over by Aunt Aurora. She would transform them and fit them to the girls.

"In those days, in Hollywood musicals (we saw them all at *el Teatro la Caridad)* and on the Cuban night club stages, it was very much in fashion to have fascinating hats and headdresses. Once my brother Pedro suggested hats along those lines for a "Begin the Beguine" number we were working on. Yet, there was nowhere to find or borrow anything like that, so we transformed lampshades into hats. We turned them upside down and hung small curtains from them, and it turned out to be a beautiful presentation. In the wings during the show, we laughed, 'look at that—that lampshade is on stage now and it's a hit!'"

Almost forty years later, Cesareo would direct the construction of a half-dozen hats based on the same idea, this time made out of papier mache, with hanging fringe, just as Rene described. They appear in the choreography for an illusion in which "Little White" the rabbit is "transformed" into a rooster.

Cesareo: "When we were in the warehouse, we decided to build a winding stairway as one of our sets. We found a large wooden crate—somebody in the neighborhood had bought a new refrigerator and thrown the crate away—and found other scrap wood to finish the project. The superintendent of public schools had let one of his teachers help me design the stairway, because he wanted to use our show to help with a fundraiser for the schools."

Rene: "At the end of the school year, when some money was made available to us, we would hire a very reputable saxophonist and a bassist to strengthen the music a bit. Manolito Campos, who played the *gallego,* was very funny. In one show, he was going to be a magician. So Mirre told him, 'Well, you have to create your own turban, and prepare your own costume.'

"So he got a swathe of white cloth and he wrapped it in such a nice way that it could pass as a turban. As the show went along, one area of the turban near his forehead became stained by the makeup as it melted, or bled, as we say. It began to appear as if it were blood-stained, and the cast started to laugh because that was not called for in the script. We had to contain ourselves to proceed with the production. When the curtain came down, everyone broke out laughing. Mirre asked, 'What are you laughing at?'

"We answered, 'Well, look at him.' The script called for a magician to enter and it turned out to be a wounded man as if he were at the front fighting in a war. We called him *el herido,* the wounded.

"Often, during the rehearsals and afterwards, we would get together and laugh at all the funny things that happened. Ultimately, everything was always under Mirre's direction. He was a leader, a true leader, and very dedicated and talented. I have never seen talent like his in all my life."

Cesareo: "Elisa loved the mazurka from the zarzuela *Luisa Fernanda* by Moreno Torroba. It is beautiful music that practically pulls you up from your seat onto the dance floor. She asked me to stage it for our show. It's done with twelve young women and twelve young men. We had parasols and beautiful ruffled hoop skirts for the women. I choreographed the number. The maidens sing of how they wish for a suitor who is sincere in his love. The men sing of the maidens' beauty, so beautiful that they can be nothing but sincere in their admiration and love. At the end, the men and women are in couples. As they turn to each other, the women dropped the parasols just enough to conceal their faces and those of their suitors. Of course the mothers and grandmothers who were chaperoning the rehearsals had to peer behind the parasols to see what was actually happening! Violeta's parents entrusted her to aunt Aurora, as did several of the other girls' parents. Aunt Aurora was highly thought of in the neighborhood.

"Those are among the happiest days of my life. What made this group so unique was our level of trust. We spoke openly to each other. There was no duplicity, there were no lies. We were honest and open with one another. What I have done since is more or less an attempt to recreate this milieu.

"We were not involved in politics. We lived our life, we sang, we danced. It is important to understand that Mirre's Follies was something extra for us in life. It was over and above our schoolwork, which we took very seriously. We were all on track to become leaders and professionals."

Rene: "When we finished *bachillerato* after five years, each of us went our own way. I went to dental school, and Mirre went to law school. Gloria's family moved to Havana where she entered business school. We used to see each other every now and then, always remembering all those years that we spent."

Cesareo: "Because the political situation was always effecting the life of everyone, all this had to disappear too. During my first year of law school in Havana, the school was closed. There were shootings on the streets and on the campuses. I witnessed some of my fellow students gunned down. I returned to Santa Clara to accept a teaching position at the Marist high school and entered the University of Las Villas to begin to study psychology and education, and eventually received my doctorate in education."

Not only did Cesareo, Rene, and the others go on to become successful professionals, but they also did it in exile, in a foreign country and in a foreign tongue, having had to begin their lives again from scratch. Rene graduated from the University of Havana and became a dentist in Santa Clara. Dominguito received his degrees in architecture and engineering in Cuba. They both married and escaped Cuba with their families—they each have four children and now, numerous grandchildren. Since an American degree was required, Rene began again and received his doctorate in dentistry from the State University of New York at Buffalo, where he has been practicing and teaching ever since. His brother Pedro, who had already emigrated to New York, was instrumental in helping him and his family settle in this country. Dominguito was incarcerated for six months in a forced labor camp before being allowed to leave Cuba. He became a university teacher and structural engineer in Chicago.

Manolito Campos became a doctor and went into exile with his family in Miami; Violeta worked as a Spanish teacher in the United States to enable one son to become a doctor and the other a judge. Gloria and her husband live in Miami Beach.

Violeta: "None of us knew what happened to Mirre, whether he got out of Cuba, or whether he was even alive. We made our inquiries and searches—Manolito especially wanted to see him, but it was not until many years later that we discovered where he was. And Manolito had already died."

Chapter Four: Kansas, Revolution, and Exile

After graduating from the *Collegio Maristas* in Santa Clara, Cesareo entered the University of Havana law school. At that time, Batista's death squads were doing away with his political opposition, which included professors and students at the university. Soon after Cesareo entered, the law school was closed by the government. In 1952 he began his studies at the *Universidad Central de Las Villas,* which had just opened its new campus in Santa Clara.

Brother Mauro, who had been a strict yet highly respected psychology teacher at the *Collegio Maristas,* was now its director. He hired Cesareo, now a student at the university, as a lay English teacher that year. Cesareo recalls, "He took a keen interest in my development. One afternoon while sitting at his desk in his office he asked me about things, and I answered such and such and so and so and poor me. He took a book from the shelves behind him, flung it at my head and rebuked me: 'Read page thirty-seven!'

"It was a psychological discussion of self-pity. It was a turning point in my life."

Mirre's Follies alumni tell how Cesareo directed shows for the school at the end of each school year. "Cesareo seemed to be more aware than most that life is often like a stage, and sometimes he would intentionally act out hilarious spoofs that would have our teacher as well as the class splitting our sides. In everything we respected him. He was a natural leader," Dominguito recalled.

39

On the occasion of his seventy-third birthday over fifty years later, the *Maristas* student alumni living in exile expressed their gratitude:

> This Magazine of MARISTANET-Saint Clara (October 2005) is dedicated to Cesareo Peláez, *El Teacher*, a Marist alumnus and our great lay teacher of English at the Santa Clara school. He worked very hard to teach us a language that soon would serve us very well, and as a coordinator of different activities he also taught to us to sing, to dance, to laugh and to be happy in our small scholastic world.
>
> Today, as a natural reflection of the great impressions that Cesareo made on us when we were young, we send a great Marist salute and a big, strong Marist hug to this GIANT of a teacher . . .

Cesareo recalled, "In 1953, during my second year in college, the Rotary club in Santa Clara was selecting a student to send to the University of Miami for a week to study politics and democracy. I was very much caught up with the question of what it means to be a Cuban, since my father was from Spain and never gave up his Spanish citizenship and my mother and her family were very Cuban. That was what my winning essay was about. Off I flew to Miami on a very small plane. This trip would cause problems with the revolution later on because I went to study democracy. During my stay in Miami, I learned about the Institute for International Education, which selected worthy individuals to study in the U.S. for one full year.

"After majoring in education and psychology for three years I received a doctorate in *Pedagogia* (education) from the *Universidad Central de Las Villas* in Santa Clara. I graduated first in my class of 800. My last year at the university I applied to the Institute for

International Education, and won a full year scholarship to the University of Kansas that included transportation, books, and food and lodging. That was around 1956. I remember telling my father of these accomplishments, and he replied, 'Mirre, these things are not reasons for real satisfaction.' He understood the difference between self-pride and the more real pleasure that comes from serving others. He had no ego, no need for looking good, and all the trappings that go with it.

"I flew to Kansas through New Orleans—my first time on a big plane—and arrived on Labor Day. I did not know what Labor Day was. Everything was closed. There were no taxis, nothing. Finally I arrived at the university, but no one else had arrived yet. Eventually, they put me in Scholarship Hall, which was a large house that the school made available to visiting and graduate students." Here he had the happy experience of democratically sharing the expenses and household tasks, preparing meals together, and all the things that make living with a number of others fun and challenging. "We all lived and worked together. That's where I discovered snow. It was nighttime, which made the white flakes against the black of the sky even more miraculous. I ran out of the dormitory practically naked and danced with the snowflakes. My roommate taught me to play football. Another student invited me for Thanksgiving to a farm, where we worked early in the morning and after dinner in the silos. That year I discovered America. My friend Hildegard taught me about dutch treat. In my culture the girls did not pay. She taught me about being American. It was a beautiful friendship.

"At the University of Kansas, my advisor was Martin Scheerer (1900-1961), who was one of the early proponents of Gestalt psychology." Scheerer had worked side by side with Max Wertheimer (1880-

41

1943), who founded Gestalt psychology, which emphasizes the importance of gestalts or 'wholes' in perception and experience. The Gestalt psychologists brought psychological thinking to new and broad frontiers, unfettered by systematization. It is said that Martin Buber's notion of "I and thou" was the single greatest influence on their thinking.

"Martin Scheerer developed the best nonverbal test in the world to measure personalities," according to Cesareo. "He directed me to take certain courses and he advised, 'Allow yourself to be thrown into the culture!' He told me to go to basketball games. They were incredible. Wilt Chamberlain was a freshman then. Two students in our dorm were in the band. So I learned the school fight song, 'I'm a jayhawker . . . onward spirit of Kansas!'"

That year at the University of Kansas Cesareo got involved in theatre. His first semester he applied for the part of the French ambassador in the Gershwin classic *Of Thee I Sing*. He didn't get the role because his accent was not French, but he made the chorus with his moving rendition of the song *Of Thee I Sing*.

By the second semester Cesareo had become friends with the director and his family, and he asked Cesareo to direct *The House of Bernarda Alba,* a Spanish drama by Lorca. As part of his direction, he taught the cast details of Spanish life, including how to hold the rosary.

At the end of the semester he needed to think about returning to Cuba. Yet he still had the summer in America, so he talked with Dr. Scheerer, who recommended that he work in the East as a counselor. Cesareo selected Greylock camp in western Massachusetts. He applied and was accepted.

"It was an extraordinary camp. After that first summer there I went to New York to Macy's and bought presents for all my friends and family in Cuba with the money I had earned as a camp counselor. Eventually all this got me in trouble with Castro's government. Many Cubans were executed or imprisoned because of their associations with the United States. When I came back to the U.S. in exile, I went to Greylock.

"Beginning with my first summer, I did theatre things for the children. The camp had a theatre. There was a student from Harvard there that summer who was a great pianist and who wrote a musical for the students. He made me Mr. Spring. I was the only adult in the show. Mr. Spring talked with a child who was very sad and cheered him up. He composed this inspirational song, the "Mr. Spring Song," which the entire cast sang with me at end of the show. I can still sing it.

"I directed the chorus. They loved me. They invited me back. And I returned for the next ten summers. I was a counselor there all through my years at Brandeis."

When he returned to Cuba, he received a position in *psychometria,* or psychometrics. He became the Director of Psychometrics for the Ministry of Education in the Province of Las Villas. Beginning in 1958, he organized intelligence testing services in public schools— the first attempt to do systematic work of this type in Cuba. In his leisure time he once again began to gather around him friends interested in theatre. The company would be called "Pegasus," after the mythological white winged horse, and arrangements were under way to build their own theatre when the final push to end the Batista dictatorship began in Santa Clara.

Since Cuba had won its independence in 1902 and adopted an extraordinarily democratic constitution based on that of the United States, its governments seemed to become mired in political ineptitude. In 1925 Gerardo Machado, a former general, was elected to its presidency. Over the next decade he created a ruthless dictatorship that, with the help of his feared Gestapo-like secret police, the Porra, imprisoned, tortured, and executed dissidents. Within a decade after his overthrow, Fulgencio Batista, another former military officer who had been popularly elected in 1940 and who returned in 1952 after staging a coup, began to establish his own dictatorship. Batista's regime was benevolent to many, yet showed a bent to the same cruel disposition toward its opposition that Machado had perfected. It had been almost six decades since the fathers of Cuba's independence had established a democratic constitution, and for practically the entire six decades the rights and liberties given to the people had been usurped by dictators. By 1958, Cubans had had enough. The rebellion against Batista promised a restoration of the constitution and a return to democratic government. Cesareo, like many others who believed in the inherent justice and necessity of this cause, worked secretly with a local underground movement to defeat Batista's army.

The turning point of the rebellion occurred in Santa Clara in December 1958. A munitions train meant to supply the army's stand against the rebels was derailed and forced to surrender. After Batista's air force bombed rebel strongholds around Santa Clara and after fierce fighting in the streets, the army surrendered to the rebels, and within days Havana fell to them as well.

Cesareo: "Batista fled Cuba on New Year's Eve. For the two weeks following January 1, 1959, while Castro made his way across Cuba to take power in Havana, the country plunged into anarchy. I was an advisor to the Boy Scouts of Santa Clara at the time and led them into the streets to help keep order. Among other things, we directed traffic. When Castro and his men paraded through Santa Clara on their way to Havana, the populace lined the route and cheered on their new leader. Cubans rejoiced and prepared for a new era of democracy. But that year, because of the anarchy, *el Dia de Reyes Magos* was not celebrated."

Cesareo continued as Director of Psychometrics for the new government, but soon enough became convinced that it was communist and that Castro had betrayed him and his countrymen. Castro's exiled daughter Alina Fernandez observed years later that her father moved so quickly and with so much efficiency to make Cuba communist "that you would think there were ten Castros."

When he received directions to send some of the best high school engineering students to communist Czechoslovakia for training— against their own wishes and those of their families—Cesareo resigned from his position with the ministry.

In the grand tradition of Machado and Batista, Castro's political police were now imprisoning, torturing and executing dissidents, members of the opposition, and anyone they considered a friend of the United States. When they targeted Cesareo, the resistance movement soon took him into its protection.

Cesareo: "Many of us went from one underground opposing Batista to another opposing Castro. But this time was different, because the new government was looking for me because of my sympathy for the United States. I made two attempts to get out of the island by boat. Both failed at the last minute. The emotions associated with these things are still very strong. Very strong. I had no idea until these recollections led me to feel them again. Cuba is an island. The only way out for us was to swim or to make our own boat."

Beginning when Batista bombed the city to quell the uprising, residents of Santa Clara had suffered bloodshed on their streets, as did the rest of Cuba. Neighbor turned against neighbor, friend against friend, brother against brother. Castro's army and police, led by the incomparable Che, did not hesitate to murder and imprison thousands of Cubans. Cesareo's best friend Samuel was machine-gunned to death while standing by his side. "I saw him lying there, riddled with bullets, bleeding from so many wounds."

One of Cesareo's students died while preparing a bomb for detonation and he saw others lying in their blood in the streets. Many of those who lived would go to prison. Political assassinations and thuggery that were common under Batista grew exponentially under the new government. The country was eviscerating itself.

"The underground got me to Havana. I remember how much fear gripped me when I entered the city. Literally, my teeth chattered. When I lay down at night on my bed, I had no idea whether I would awake. I am alive today because of the resistance. Their story should be told: their loyalty, effectiveness, their leadership, and the many who fell."

Cesareo describes the resistance as an example of true anarchy in the highest sense of the word, that is, one freely chooses to grant authority to whoever one believes deserves it, or not to grant it at all. "The resistance had no formal government. It was responsive to the needs of the moment. Leadership was by consensus. Sometimes there were no leaders. We cooperated to do what needed to be done."

Within a week after the tragic Bay of Pigs fiasco, Brother Mauro, the director of the Marist school where Cesareo had taught, helped him escape by disguising him as a priest, so that he could gain admission to the Colombian embassy—a safe haven. As he entered, true to his costumed role, he pronounced a blessing on Castro's military police who were guarding the embassy's gates.

"Then there were only six or possibly nine of us seeking asylum in the embassy. Over the next weeks ten more came, then another ten or twelve, then another, another, until after a month or so (I lost track of time) there were sixty-five. Some time later, it could have been weeks, it could have been months, some arrangement was made between the Colombian prime minister and Castro; they arranged to provide him with something he wanted in exchange for us. Then one day they called us all into the main hall, where they have receptions, and read the names of those who had been granted permission to leave. Two would not. Of the sixty-three who would, my name was read sixty-second. There was silence in the room during the reading and after. Silence. The tension and relief were unspeakable.

"The Colombian government sent an Avianca airplane. We were transported from the embassy right onto the tarmac at the Havana airport in the official embassy car with little Columbian flags flying from its fenders. The consul himself escorted us on each trip. The car held only five passengers, so he had to make many runs. When we got to the airport, a red carpet was unrolled from the door of the car right to the stairway leading onto the plane. The compound, car, carpet and plane were all Colombian territory. The Cuban officials couldn't touch us.

. . .

47

"Walking the gauntlet of the carpet, crowds of people were throwing eggs at us and shouting *'Gusanos!'* ['worms'—Castro's denunciation of émigrés] and other foul curses from a balcony overlooking the tarmac. Ever since that departure, I have resisted saying goodbye to anyone."

"I was the fifth or sixth person on board the plane. I moved toward the back and took my seat. When everyone was on board, silence again. We were forced to wait on the runway for hours. Finally the plane received clearance and we took off. Then after some time, the pilot announced to us: 'We have just left the territorial waters of Cuba. You are free.'

"Some people cried. Some applauded. I sat silently. The pain was unbearable. The faces of my friends who had been murdered or who had disappeared passed before me. I thought of all the others, perhaps thousands, who had not been able to get out and who might perish. The most fortunate would lose everything and face exile.

"We flew to Mexico, where all but three of us disembarked. We stopped again in Costa Rica to refuel. When the plane arrived in Colombia, there was no one to meet me. I had nothing and nowhere to go.

"I had not recalled many of these details about the embassy. Reading a book recently about a woman's recollections of leaving Cuba as a teenager aboard the Mariel boatlift brought me back to them. Once again I experienced the agonies that eventually subsided into an inextinguishable ache. The island that I knew and loved is gone forever. Literally, there is nothing to return to. What lay in store for me, as for every exile, was grief for the lives and country we had lost. However its poignancy may be reduced by time and triumph, this grief remains for the rest of your life. In the words of Herman Melville, 'It is not down in any map; true places never are.'"

Mirre at 26 years old.

Fiesta Motel

RESTAURANT — COCKTAIL LOUNGE
ROUTE 2 — BOX 120
PORT ALLEN, LA.

Dear Conan

Let me know how you are getting on. Did your project work out? Sorry I was in such a hurry when I left that I had no time to listen.

Verna will know where to reach me. I'll probably stay in Puerto Rico for a time. If I do I'll practice my Spanish.

Buena suerte

Abe Maslow

"You Can Have Fun at the Fiesta"

A note from Maslow in his last year.

Chapter Five: With Abraham Maslow

Cesareo's academic credentials qualified him for a professorship of psychology at *Pontificia Universidad Javeriana* in Bogotá, where he taught from September 1961 to June 1962. He recalled:

It was becoming increasingly clear that the political situation in Colombia was not all that different from Cuba. I saw many signs of instability and a threatening rebel movement, so at the end of the academic year I sought admission to the United States. I recall arriving for my appointment with the United States consul in Bogotá and waiting in the reception area. Eventually the secretary asked me for my passport, which I gave her. A moment later I was called into the consul's office. I sat in front of his desk and he asked me for my passport. I told him that I did not have it, and before I could get another word out of my mouth he launched into a tirade: "What do you mean you do not have a passport? How do you expect to get anywhere without one? And here you sit wasting my time! Who do you think you are? And do you know where you are? This is the United States Consulate!"

I interrupted him to tell him politely in a quiet tone, "Sir, excuse me, but your secretary asked me for it when I arrived. She has it now, I believe."

He felt so embarrassed by his conduct that he asked the secretary to bring my passport to him and immediately stamped and signed the authorization for my visa.

When my plane took off from Bogotá, I was overwhelmed and cried for hours. It seemed that my life up to this moment amounted to zero. Coming to the States meant having to start all over again.

He began again with everything he had—extraordinary intelligence, a soul on fire, and some basic English. As his father had gone to Cuba penniless and without family, so, too, Cesareo entered his new homeland.

When he arrived in the United States, he went to the offices of Graylock in New York City. They arranged for him to go to camp before the season opened and help set things up for the summer. When the campers arrived, he was there to welcome them. "That summer, while accompanying myself on the guitar singing *Siempre en mi Corazon,* a beautiful Cuban song, I became very sad," Cesareo recalls. "It is a love song, but suddenly the lyrics began to speak to me about Cuba: *Estas en mi corazon aunque estoy lejos de ti, y es el tormento mayor de esta fatal separacion* ('You are in my heart, though I am far from you, and that is the greatest torment of this fated separation')." Greylock eventually had a wooden sign carved at the campfire grounds that read, "Cesareo's place."

After the camp season ended, he was offered a position by the father of one of the campers, who owned a furniture factory in Keene, New Hampshire. He worked there for about three months. "The owner gave me a very good job as his assistant, but it was mostly out of affection for me and my work as a counselor. There was not much for me to do for his company, and his employees began to be jealous of me," Cesareo recalled.

"Miraculously a temporary position teaching Spanish at the local high school opened. The teacher had been called back to Spain to resolve family difficulties, and for four months I taught the class. After school I would return to the furniture factory. One evening after work, I was researching something at the town library, and I asked the librarian for some psychology journals. She answered no, she would not get them for me, because they were only for real Americans, or some such phrase, which precluded someone with a foreign accent like myself from using them."

"That night I could not sleep. It was impossible to replant myself in another Cuban community in the United States—New York, Miami, or wherever. I needed to begin again. It must have been about four in the morning when I wrote to Dr. Abraham Maslow, who was for me America's leading psychologist and visionary. I had read *Motivation and Personality* in Cuba about five years earlier. He was teaching at Brandeis University, in Waltham, Massachusetts. I asked him to accept me as a student. He responded, 'Meet me at the Brown faculty office building, Room 102, on December 20 at 10:00.' I started the night before and hitchhiked from New Hampshire to Cambridge in a snow storm. The next morning I got to Brandeis in time for the interview.

"The secretary of the psychology department informed me that Professor Maslow was in Washington, D.C. He was president of the American Psychological Association and was attending a conference. I turned away from her to hide my tears. Then she continued.

53

Arrangements had been made for Dr. James Klee, another member of the faculty, to see me.

"Dr. Klee was a big man with a trim white beard who taught existential psychology. He invited me into his office. Since my credentials, academic records, and other papers usually required for admission were lost forever in Cuba, the Brandeis faculty could only draw on my records with the Institute for International Education and my year at Kansas."

Dr. Klee told Cesareo that Professor Maslow's next seminar would be held on Saturday mornings and asked where he was living. When Cesareo answered "Keene, New Hampshire," Dr. Klee informed him that he would need to find a job in the area, because it was just too far to commute from Keene. As their meeting drew to a close, he suggested that Cesareo check the bulletin board down the hall. A number of jobs being offered to Brandeis graduate students were posted there. Cesareo left Dr. Klee's office and walked down the hall to the board. Among the offers was one as a principal for a South Weymouth, Massachusetts, school for people who at that time were classified as "the educable mentally retarded."

Elisa's first child was a daughter who had been born with these disabilities and had died as an infant. This was in the midst of the street fighting in Santa Clara during the revolution. With the help of their capable housekeeper, Cesareo had taken charge of the child's care. He learned about her difficulties first hand. The school hired him; the advance they provided allowed Cesareo to purchase a car to commute to Waltham from South Weymouth.

. . .

54

Cesareo spent that Christmas alone in South Weymouth. His dinner consisted of a pizza; afterwards he went to a movie down the block. *The Sound of Music* was playing: "I was the only person in the theatre. I remember when the lyrics, 'Bless my homeland forever,' came, I began to cry and cry."

The second semester at Brandeis began in the third week of January. On that Saturday morning, after Cesareo's first graduate seminar, Professor Maslow brought him back to his house for lunch prepared by his wife Bertha. From then on he had lunch with them every Saturday. The Maslows became his family. He began to feel at home there.

Since Abe and Bertha were Jewish, they did not celebrate Christmas. However, the next year, Maslow had one of his doctoral candidates invite Cesareo to his house to share Christmas with him and his wife. And he arranged for them to have Cesareo telephone Elisa in Cuba and paid for the call.

"My interest in studying humanistic psychology with Maslow coincided with my deepest needs," Cesareo said. "The phrase, 'doctor, heal thyself,' applied to me. At that point in my life, it was absolutely necessary to allow for a reconstruction of my own psychology on a new footing. Unless you have experienced these things, they may make no sense to you. My sorrow, pain and sense of loss were immitigable."

"Although there were Spanish-speaking students and faculty at the university, I immersed myself with English-speaking friends. As a result, I stopped speaking Spanish entirely. Months and years passed without my speaking a word of it. I began to develop an amnesia of sorts about my Spanish-speaking past. And I began to dream in

English. Sometimes in conversation with Maslow I would struggle with the pronunciation of an English word. Maslow would not correct me by saying, 'the proper pronunciation is . . .' Rather, he said, 'Cesareo, that's all right. And some people pronounce it . . ."

Cesareo threw himself into his new life with all his intensity. In those first months at Brandeis he also helped settle Elisa, her husband, and new-born son in nearby Brockton. The Catholic Charities of Massachusetts, which was highly responsive to the needs of recent immigrants, assisted with their expenses.

In late spring a neighbor found Cesareo collapsed in the hallway of his apartment building. He awoke in Quincy Hospital. The nurse told him that Abe had already come to visit. The doctor informed Professor Maslow that Cesareo was suffering from the late stages of pneumonia due to overwork and malnutrition. Maslow had left a gift for him with the nurse. It was a collection of cartoons from the *New Yorker* magazine. Maslow immediately arranged for Cesareo to get a residence counselorship in the freshman quadrangle.

"As a residence counselor, I could eat good food in the cafeteria, have a place to live on campus and even receive a stipend for books. It enabled me to take a full four-course graduate study program," Cesareo recalled. "A long time before post-traumatic stress syndrome became a common diagnosis, Maslow understood what had happened to me and what I needed."

Cesareo returned to Graylock that summer. His safe haven once again welcomed him and provided a less strenuous work load to allow him to heal in the summer beauty of the Berkshires.

Cesareo immersed himself in understanding the intricacies of Maslow's psychology—a kind of self-initiation. That fall semester of 1963 he became Maslow's teaching assistant and led sections twice a week based on the professor's lectures. He made a mark at Brandeis by his ability to explain Maslow's most difficult ideas in terms that students completely understood, and in language that was inspiring and uplifting. As a result, being in his classroom was a transformational experience for many.

Maslow lectured from the right side of the stage to an auditorium full of students; Cesareo sat on stage left. Very often the professor spoke to Cesareo on stage, or audibly consulted with him. Clearly he was fond of Cesareo and considered him to be his "right hand," his representative, his interpreter, his protege. The freshman class was housed in one quadrangle and dined in a single refectory. The underclassmen spent many meals at Cesareo's table in spirited discussions about Maslow's theories of self-actualization.

The Brandeis community was a highly charged intellectual and social environment. The freshmen admired Cesareo. His company provided respite from academic pressures, good counsel, friendship and inspiration. One spring afternoon, at the height of the popularity of Anthony Quinn's movie depiction of the irrepressibly exuberant Zorba the Greek, Cesareo led an impromptu *Miserlou* around the pond at the center of the freshman quad, dozens of students following in a circle, eventually breaking into joyous dancing. In the midst of an academy that throbbed with intellect, his example reminded students that exuberance and *joie de vivre* were necessary to a full life.

Practically everyone who came into contact with him sensed there was something special about him: an extraordinary sensitivity to people and an intuitive Sherlock Holmesian sense of observation.

One sunny spring afternoon I was chatting with him by the pond at the center of the freshman quadrangle, with its three dormitory buildings and student center surrounding us. Cesareo began to move his feet about, shifting weight from one to the other. Suddenly I noticed that Cesareo was mirroring my own unconscious fidgeting. For the first time in my life I became aware that I was moving that way. Surprise melted into gratitude that Cesareo had brought it to my attention in such a playful manner.

When he encountered a student, which was usually with a warm, receptive smile, it seemed that Cesareo was asking himself, "What does this person want for himself? What can I say or offer him that will be helpful? How can I support him, back him, endorse him?"

He spared no effort in discharging his responsibilities as residence counselor. His door was always open. He would read students' papers to offer constructive suggestions, such as being less dogmatic: "Consider using the word 'perhaps,' or the phrase 'it may be that.'" He was fundamentally accessible, fun to be with, sought after, and enormously intelligent. Something about him was always the teacher, the intellectual seeker and leader, keenly aware of the group dynamics of the people he was with.

Although Cesareo would speak of his past with some of his colleagues and faculty, students knew practically nothing of his background. He spoke with an accent, perhaps some detected it was Cuban, but most did not. His conversation never mentioned the island. None of the freshmen (nor did most Americans of the time, one might venture) had any idea of how the events in Cuba had torn families' lives apart, how many people were imprisoned, tortured and executed because of their suspected ties to the United States, how a highly educated and cultured class was forced into homeless and penniless exile, and how many of them were unable to get out alive or lost their lives at sea while fleeing.

In one of life's ironic and malicious twists, a romanticized and fictionalized Che Guevara had become a hero to many of the students on American university campuses in the 1960s, and Brandeis was no exception. Castro's deft manipulation of the American media made it possible for him to export an image of Che as a hero of the revolutionary culture, and American college students in particular bought it. But Cesareo had helplessly witnessed Che the cold-blooded executioner first hand

"I learned at Brandeis to be silent about Cuba. Even faculty members praised Castro's ascendancy. There was only one option available, under those circumstances—silence. Maslow understood, though. He never asked me about Cuba. I spoke to him from time to time about some things. He understood; even without words, he understood."

One day Cesareo's father surprised everyone with a call from Boston's Logan airport to the psychology department. Constantino had just arrived and wanted to find Cesareo to help him settle in the area. That very day Cesareo found an envelope in his campus mailbox. In it was a check for $1,000 and note that read, "In case this might help. [signed] Abe."

"Meanwhile I was still struggling with English fluency; I studied Maslow's *Toward a Psychology of Being* every moment I could in order to learn how to express ideas in his magnificent psychological language. The requirements of the residence counselorship and looking after my freshmen, working as Maslow's teaching assistant, my off-campus work as a school principal, and of course, my own studies kept me riveted in the present."

The linchpin of Maslow's work since the late 1940s was his study of psychological health. He was perhaps the first to focus on and explore the nature of self-actualizing individuals. He brought to his work an enormous philosophical breadth—ranging from Buddhist thought to William James, to Freud and his students and beyond.

When Cesareo arrived at Brandeis, Maslow had just returned from California, where he had begun to apply his psychology of human health and self-actualization to the management of a nascent Silicon Valley manufacturing facility. Back at Brandeis, he enthusiastically began to share his management theories with his students. "What a surprise," Cesareo recalled. "The graduate students in our seminar had been expecting him to discuss his hierarchy of needs and his popular theories of motivation. Instead, he began the semester by explaining that the improvement of mankind through individual work, such as psychotherapy, would not occur. Pursuing these ends through the workplace was more practical because individual growth is determined to a large extent by social conditions. If you want self-actualizing people, you need self-actualizing workplaces. In this way we were introduced to the theories of management he was formulating."

Maslow was the first to enunciate the principle of synergy, that is, a business, like any group, functions best when it is composed of self-actualizing people for whom there is no dichotomy between selfishness and unselfishness. Maslow explained that where there is a true regard for another person, his happiness is mine; synergy has occurred "when the happiness of the other person makes me happy, or when I enjoy the self-actualization of the other as much as I do my own, or when the differentiation between the word 'other' and the words 'my own' has disappeared."

Maslow firmly believed that a business environment, to be truly good for people, must be based on trust. Management, he posited, is good for people when it understands that they wish to be trusted and to trust. This is basic to the creation of a healthy workplace. More than that, a trusting environment encourages people to trust themselves, their hunches, and intuitions, and ultimately to be sensitive to their inner lives. Trust is synergic. The better I am for myself, the more I can be for others. As the sage Hillel said over 2000 years ago, "If I am not for myself, then who will be for me? And if I am for myself alone, then what am I?"

It may be that Maslow's ultimate concern was with values. How can the workplace provide conditions that foster the pursuit of truth, beauty, goodness, justice, and mercy? Good citizens, healthy, responsible, self-actualizing people are the ones best prepared and most apt to love and pursue the great virtues.

Maslow believed that "the American dynamic" was democratic rather than aristocratic. To be democratic means that American management is not based on "pull." To rise to a position of leadership one does not need a well-placed relative or hereditary privileges or to have attended a particular school. "It all depends on your own capability and talents."

He was very aware that his personal story could not have happened in any other country: "My father was an immigrant. I was brought up in the slums of New York City. I am a sidewalk boy who has gone on to a marvelous vocation."

He used to ask his students how they could tell whether a business or any group was functioning well. The answer: "Find out how often they have parties."

Not long before his death he participated in a management retreat for a national corporation. At its conclusion he shared his observations with the managers: "I think it might be helpful . . . to simply become more aware of our good fortune and our plain luck in being part of this American dynamic. Why? Because individually we do not 'deserve' our heritage of freedom, vast natural resources, national political maturity, or managerial skill . . . I feel grateful and privileged to be an American, and I suggest that you do too."

In his introduction to an unpublished manuscript entitled *Reflections of Abraham Maslow,* Cesareo writes,

> The optimism inherent in Maslow's view of mankind is particularly obvious in his notion of the inner nature: people are basically good or neutral rather than evil; there is in everyone an impulse toward growth and the fulfillment of potentials; psychopathology is the result of the twisting and frustration of the essential nature of the human organism.
>
> Maslow sees life as an endless struggle to grow and to reach one's full potential. For growth to occur, the inner nature must have an adequate opportunity to express itself, it is the psychologically healthy and growth-motivated people who are willing to endure the pain necessary to allow their inner nature to express itself. On the other hand, psychologically unhealthy people permit their nature to be easily overcome by the evils of society. Maslow believed that

more useful information about human nature could be derived by attempting to determine how people become more psychologically healthy, than could ever be derived by focusing on ways of making people unsick. When reading Maslow, one is reminded of the poet's comment, "We are all born in the gutter, but some of us choose to look at the stars." Maslow believed that a person's private, subjective experience is what determines behavior. External reality is only a set of circumstances and one with which subjective reality, reality as it is perceived by the individual, doesn't always coincide. When the two do coincide, there is only a partial match. He wrote: "First of all and most important of all is the strong belief that man has an essential nature of his own. Second, there is involved the conception that fully healthy and normal and desirable development consists of actualizing this nature, in fulfilling these potentialities, and in developing into maturity along the lines that this hidden, covert, dimly seen essential nature dictates, growing from within rather than being shaped from without."

As soon as he completed it, Maslow gave Cesareo a typewritten copy of his preface to the revised edition of *Toward a Psychology of Being,* about to be published in 1968. There he wrote:

I must confess that I have come to think of this humanist trend in psychology as a revolution in the truest, oldest sense of the word, the sense in which Galileo, Darwin, Einstein, Freud, or Marx made revolutions, i.e., new ways of perceiving and thinking, new images of man and of society, new conceptions of ethics and of values, new directions in which to move.

This Third Psychology is now one facet of a general Weltanschauung, a new philosophy of life, a new conception of man, the beginning of a new century of work (that is, of course, if we can meanwhile manage to hold off a holocaust). For any man of good will ... there is work to be done here, effective, virtuous, satisfying work which can give rich meaning to one's own life and to others.

This psychology is not purely descriptive or academic. It suggests action and implies consequences. It helps to generate a way of life, not only for the person himself within his own private psyche, but also for the same person as a social being, a member of society. As a matter of fact, it helps us to realize how interrelated these two aspects of life really are. Ultimately, the best "helper" is the "good person." So often the sick or inadequate person, trying to help, does harm instead.

I should say also that I consider Humanistic, Third Force Psychology to be transitional, a preparation for a still "higher" Fourth Psychology, transpersonal, transhuman, centered in the cosmos rather than in human needs and interest, going beyond humanness, identity, self-actualization and the like.

No matter how high his thinking could soar, Maslow kept his camel well tethered. Perhaps one of the reasons his work has endured is his recognition of the reality of evil and the dark side of human nature. Cesareo recalls, "He used to tell me, 'Cesareo, if you ever write a book on psychology, make sure you make the second chapter on envy and the third on jealousy.'"

As a Teaching Fellow and graduate PhD candidate in Psychology at Brandeis, Cesareo also studied with Dr. James B. Klee, Dr. Ricardo B. Morant, and Dr. George Kelly. Associated with the faculty was Dr. Eugenia Hanfmann, the courageous director of Brandeis' pioneer Psychological Counseling Center. In addition, the lingering influence of leading gestalt psychologists Dr. Kurt Goldstein (who died in 1965) and Dr. Andreas Angyal (who had recently moved to a teaching hospital) shaped the orientation of the department. It was perhaps the finest psychology department in the United States at that time.

Cesareo continued to study and teach with Maslow without preparing a formal PhD thesis because he had already received a doctorate in Cuba. He believed that he would soon return to Cuba to resume a leadership position in the government once the communists were toppled. "My thinking was, 'who wants a degree when next year we'll be back in Cuba?' Every Cuban in America believed that next Christmas we would be home. The 14,000 children of Operation Peter Pan were sent from Cuba because their parents thought it was going to be for one year, a year and a half, maybe. Not ten, twenty, thirty, forty years." Eventually however it became apparent to him that waiting for Castro to fall was a waste of time. So he applied for U.S. citizenship.

Cesareo was sworn a United States citizen in 1967 in Lowell, Massachusetts. The secretary of the Brandeis psychology department served as his witness. When he next went to the Solomon Mental Health Center in Lowell, where he was working as a psychotherapist, the staff and clients were waiting for him with a cake decorated with the stars and stripes. At the party, one of the clients exclaimed, "How can it be? You've become a citizen but you still have your accent?" Cesareo recalls that her therapy worked wonders. They stayed in contact for years.

Knowing Cesareo's interest in group psychology, and sensing his natural abilities to lead, Maslow arranged for Cesareo to attend the National Training Laboratories (NTL) summer program in Bethel, Maine. NTL was at the forefront of research into group dynamics and the development of new models of social interaction. In fact, NTL practically invented T-groups and encounter groups. One of the founders of NTL was Kurt Lewin (1890-1947), an exile from Nazi Germany, who pioneered the field of group processes. His thinking was influenced by the work of Wertheimer and the early Gestalt psychologists.

Maslow also sent Cesareo to work with Jacob Moreno (1889-1974), one of the century's unsung geniuses, who single-handedly founded what we know as group therapy, sociometry, and psychodrama.

With a group of teenage friends in the first decade of twentieth century Vienna, at a time when psychoanalysis was becoming prominent, Moreno established *Stegreiftheater* (theatre of spontaneity) for young children, displaced persons, troubled adolescents, and prisoners. His theatre company was made up of his friends. They did their work for its own sake and took no fees.

After studying medicine and psychiatry, he emigrated to the United States in 1925. His students in the 1930s and '40s included Fritz Perls, Eric Berne, and Karl Menninger. The editorial board of his journal *Sociometry* was composed of many leading social thinkers, including John Dewey, Gardner Murphy, Margaret Mead, George Gallup and Kurt Lewin.

In 1940 Moreno founded his institute in Beacon, New York, that became the premier psychodrama treatment facility. Psychodrama is based on the idea that encounter (rather than psychoanalytic transference) is the effective principle of cure. For the neurotic and even for the healthy individual seeking personal growth, psychodrama is an invitation to self-liberation with immense and exhilarating power. More than anyone, Moreno was aware of its potency. He wrote that we are liable to "fear our own spontaneity as our ancestors feared fire. The aim of these sundry techniques is not to turn the subjects into actors, but rather to stir them up to be on the stage what they are, more deeply and explicitly than they appear to be in life."

The point of it all is to bring what is learned into one's daily life, which can be seen as a series of encounters, of opportunities to experience others in all their richness and complexity, and to respond to them from the fullest sense of oneself. Jacob Moreno's broad and intellectually exciting and satisfying system touches on all levels of experience, including cosmology, ethics, aesthetics, and ontology. And it all hangs together in a psychological system that equals Freud's in terms of its inner coherence and completeness, but is much more positive and filled with hope and promise.

The essence of Moreno's seminal writing lies in the idea that groups have an internal life of their own and that this life can best be understood by examining the choices members make at any given moment with regard to each other. He insisted that every group has underneath its visible structure an internal, invisible structure that is "real, alive, and dynamic." Furthermore, Moreno believed that every group has the capacity for a transcendent interconnectedness among its members. This state of being attuned to one another can rarely be accomplished, however, without skillful management.

In recent decades a number of studies have demonstrated conclusively that people live healthier, happier and longer lives when they are intimately connected to friends and family. Comradeship, being valued as a friend, brother, or as a member of a club, group, ensemble, congregation are necessary for a healthy life. They reduce stress, decrease susceptibility to disease, and are part and parcel of being a deeply-experiencing, wisdom-loving and inclusive and encompassing type of individual. Conversely, isolation and loneliness have been found to be risk factors for disease. From this point of view, Jacob Moreno was way ahead of his time. By the 1930s, he had clearly documented the positive effect that "good group belongingness" (to use Maslow's phrase) has for people. As members of families or groups of friends and associates at work, people can help make one another healthier, or they can detract from this. This is one way of understanding Moreno's view that "encounter" is what cures people. The extent to which we can experience one another with the unencumbered innocence of a child and respond to one another with the surprising authentic expressiveness of which we are capable— in short, how we encounter one another—determines the water in which we swim psychologically.

. . .

"Jacob Moreno is one of the greatest geniuses of group work. He hasn't gotten the praise or recognition he deserves," according to Cesareo. "His psychodrama is extraordinary, but it's not only psychodrama. His expertise is also in group processes. I used to go to his institute in New York on weekends. I'd leave Brandeis on Friday night and return Monday morning, spending the weekend with the Morenos, living in their house. Sometimes I would spend two weeks with them in Beacon. Often they took me to their public performances of psychodrama in Manhattan on Saturday night. Many times I directed. His wife, Zirka, who led the institute with Jacob, was fascinated with my abilities to direct. I was a natural, and the Morenos saw that very clearly. That is how I became the president of the American Psychodrama Society, and in all honesty, I think there was no other person who could direct the psychodrama as well as I. Now I sometimes do it *in situ,* in real life, to help someone work something through. I still do things like that. It's part of group work."

Maslow's associate, Dr. George Kelly, had recommended Cesareo for the position as principal psychologist at the Solomon Mental Health Center in Lowell, Massachusetts. It was the first center in the state to take the mentally ill out of hospitals and put them in houses. Its director, Dr. Bachoven, understood Cesareo's approach to therapy and supported him completely. He built a psychodrama theatre just for Cesareo in the basement of the center, complete with theatrical lighting. He asked Cesareo to begin with sessions with the nurses to help them develop a sense of community.

In 1969, Maslow had decided to leave Brandeis and return to California where he had been offered a liberal fellowship by a leading technology entrepreneur. It was an opportunity to work and write as he pleased.

During one of his prior trips to California, Maslow had happened upon Esalen, which practically overnight had become the wellspring for the human potential movement on the West Coast. Maslow's theories of self-actualization deeply influenced the founders of Esalen and they welcomed him heartily. He was impressed with the way Esalen's staff was opening psychology to Eastern thought and with their humanist bent. But, there was much about the atmosphere there with which he did not agree.

Esalen embodied and radiated the new zeitgeist of liberation. It was in the air on college campuses in the 1960s, and you got it without having to attend encounter groups or sensitivity training sessions. At Brandeis, the counterculture was mainstream. The university had always encouraged freedom of expression and individual liberty. Supreme Court Justice Louis Dembitz Brandeis, its namesake, fought for laws to protect exploited men and women in the workplace, resisted the curtailment of freedom of speech which had been threatened after the outbreak of World War I, and believed steadfastly in the enlightened attitudes of the authors of the Constitution.

It was this milieu of courageous intellectual liberty that had attracted Maslow to join Brandeis' faculty. Yet he was not impressed by the looseness of the new popular culture that was developing. Liberty can be abused and does not excuse ill-conceived behavior.

It was with Maslow's encouragement that Cesareo had begun to think about a center on the East Coast that would sanely and responsibly offer encounter, T-group sessions, and psychodrama. It might be a place where humanistic principles of management as well as Eastern disciplines could be explored within a milieu that retained a respect for the most wholesome American traditions.

Chapter Six: Cumbres

A wealthy New England entrepreneur had been impressed with Cesareo's lectures and demonstrations at the 1968 national convention of the American Psychodrama Society, of which he was president. He offered financial support for Cesareo's idea for a center. After other investors had come on board, the search began for a property to house the center. They looked at a large castle for sale in Gloucester, Massachusetts, and at one of the wharves in downtown Boston, which at that time contained abandoned warehouses and could be purchased reasonably.

Finally they learned that the Inn in Dublin, New Hampshire, was for sale. It was a ninety-five-acre property within sight of Mt. Monadnock. The main building offered a foyer, living rooms, dining rooms, and hotel kitchen below, with guest rooms above. Spread in the shade of elms and oaks were several outbuildings containing meeting rooms and additional living quarters. Beyond a greenhouse, a garden, and a rolling lawn were woodlands with a stream running through.

The center, which opened in April 1969, was called *Cumbres,* a Spanish word meaning the point were the earth meets the sky— "peaks." Some of Maslow's former students joined him as staff. This was both a blessing and a curse: They were well-prepared for the work, but none of them ever developed a real loyalty to Cesareo.

. . .

Cumbres may be described as a place of discovery where new ways of understanding the world and oneself could appear. Its brochure stated:

Within each of us
there is the power to grow;
to be more effective;
to better relate with others;
to find greater satisfaction
in everything we do.
Cumbres is an environment
for growth;
an experience for everyone
to enjoy, to profit by.
In an unhurried atmosphere,
within pleasant surroundings,
it encourages contemplation
while enriching the
healthy conflicts
which are the steps
to understanding ourselves.

A description of "imaginative problem solving" reads:

Business and professional men
must work effectively with others
to plan, to solve problems,
and to efficiently carry out
projects and programs.
We can learn how we work with
others to solve specific problems,
and to carry out their solutions.
We can learn to understand
how we approach our work and
how others react to our methods.
We can learn how to use
our strengths to create
better working relationships.

The sentence "We can learn to understand how we approach our work and how others react to our methods" is central to how Cesareo tends to think about things. He often says that our attitude towards our work determines its results or effects, and it influences how others respond to us. In the same way, you need to be a friend, and be perceived as a friend, if you wish to have a friend.

Robert Taylor, the *Boston Globe's* chief book critic for decades, came to Cumbres in 1970 to attend a weekend of lectures by Professor Liu Da, a sage and master of the *I Ching, Book of Changes.* Liu Da taught law and philosophy in Taiwan and was a member of the Taiwanese section at the United Nations. Mr. Taylor was attracted to forms of thought that insisted on the widest range of human possibilities. "At Cumbres one seeks responsible freedom," he wrote. "[It is] an oasis of rural solitude where everyday people may encounter their not-so-mundane selves—sometimes through sensitivity group work . . . sometimes through the development of meditative powers and body language; sometimes through the study of environment and problem-solving. And sometimes outside the logical structure of Western thought."

When Cesareo told a reporter from the *New York Times* that the staff were sober Republican types, and that their values were more like those of a monastery, perhaps he was saying that at Cumbres marital fidelity and other traditional values were encouraged. The reporter described Cesareo as a "charismatic personality" who was seeking to establish an environment that went beyond the traditional methods of teaching human development; Cumbres was a place where healthy persons could "live together and develop their inherent spirituality."

The *New York Times* article noted that seventeen full-time paid staff lived there. Unlike other popular growth centers of that time, Cumbres owned its own property. It was perhaps the only center whose staff not only led workshops and taught courses, but shared in the daily administrative tasks from washing the dishes to keeping the books.

The article is titled, "Commune Built by Republican Types." Although the reporter called it a commune (a popular word in 1970), the article backpedals as it goes along, noting that Cumbres' life-style is basic American: people are paid for their work and families live together in their own homes.

The article describes the daily T'ai chi exercise and meditation classes led by a resident seventy-three-year-old Chinese master as an example of the center's openness to spiritual traditions. Teachers from other spiritual paths were brought to Cumbres to teach and lecture as well. It attracted corporate presidents, cultural leaders, writers, housewives, students, teachers—basically people who were already healthy, responsible citizens and who sensed that there was a greater potential to be explored. The *Times* summed up Cumbres as "a growth center to help put middle-class Americans in better touch with their feelings, other persons and the world around them."

A writer for *Look Magazine* described Cumbres as "a retreat where one can come to get in touch with himself and with others, for a [psychological] tune-up . . . Cesareo Pelaez, 38, father of Cumbres, believes in the routine—almost a ritual—of living together, and visitors fall into the community schedule: garden work, household chores, yoga, art, meditation seminars and T'ai chi."

The author notes that Cesareo is Cumbres and describes him as "a psychologist who has used sensory awareness and psychodrama," who "now prefers to work more intuitively with groups, letting things 'grow organically.'" Cesareo is quoted, "My goal is to get at the essence of the individual without getting trapped in incidentals."

He continued to put his psychotherapeutic skills to work to solve problems for friends and friends of friends, without remuneration. He had a knack for setting people straight without doing injury. In many cases their gratitude lasted a lifetime. More than one member of his future magic company received his help during these years. Psychotherapist Fritz Perls once stated that there are only two kinds of people: nurturing and poisonous. Cesareo is the former, and his ventures with people, such as Cumbres and the Cabot Street Cinema Theatre, are also nurturing.

Elisa had taken up residence at Cumbres with her husband and young son, having moved from their apartment in Brockton. She loved Cumbres.

Cumbres lasted barely eighteen months before Cesareo decided to close it. Its staff had begun to diverge from its disciplined values, and some differences with its investors had begun to surface.

"I brought a beautiful tent and we erected it on the grounds in the summer so we could do shows with magic and masks, and we brought a faculty member from Brandeis who used to teach mask-making and the language of metaphor. The tent was taken to the famous Woodstock concert, against my deepest wishes, and after it got destroyed, something changed."

The decision to close Cumbres was courageous. Cesareo stood alone. He announced his intention to close less than six months after

Abraham Maslow's sudden death: "For the second time in my life, I cried and cried and could not stop crying for hours. Again I had ended at zero."

The staff and students at Cumbres did not see evidence of his sorrow. He understood very well that life requires one to be a good actor. To those around him, he continued to be the uplifting leader. Many Cumbres alumni and staff kept contact with him. Some joined his nascent theatre company half a dozen years later. Even forty years later, others continue to keep in touch. At the end, all the investors got their money back. Before closing he made sure that every member of the staff had a job. Many went to work for the investors' companies. Around Thanksgiving time, Cesareo invited several members of his staff to accompany him to Europe after Cumbres closed in December. Two Amherst College sophomores accepted. He had met Webster Bull in the spring of 1970, and his roommate Tom that fall. They were among the students and faculty from the surrounding colleges that Cumbres had attracted. For a nominal fee students could attend a college student series, consisting of Tuesday and Thursday evening seminars and workshops. Some, especially those endowed with a zest for life and a thirst for understanding and who showed leadership potential, were invited for weekends and eventually offered internships. He found two in Webster and Tom. Like most Cumbres attendees, they were exhilarated by their experience there. To Cesareo they were the two most promising lights of the group.

For Webster and Tom, being with Cesareo in Europe gave their inner compasses a true north—his life was a model for being awake and fully alive. Putting Cumbres behind him, Cesareo sold his car, gathered his cash, took his two new friends under his wing, and boarded their flight to the continent.

Chapter Seven: Beginnings

Four months later, while they were traveling in Spain, Tom began to feel pressure from his parents to continue his studies at Amherst College in the fall. A registration notice from his selective service board sealed his premature return to America. Cesareo and Webster continued on, studying ballet, mime, and Morris sword dancing. They saw European circuses, theatrical revues such as the Follies Bergères, Shakespeare plays, puppet theatre and stage magic. Cesareo was Webster's teacher and friend. Webster wrote in retrospect, "The five months that remained to us were maybe the richest period, day for day, moment for moment, of my life."

Their reading included the work of George Ivanovitch Gurdjieff (1877?-1949). His was perhaps the most compelling psychology that Cesareo had encountered. "I had studied Freud, Jung, Adler and Horney. It became clear to me that, theoretically and practically, Gurdjieff's psychology embraced all the others, and even offered more," Cesareo states.

Gurdjieff, a Greek-Armenian, has exerted a considerable influence on contemporary psychological and religious thinking. Those who knew him mention his extraordinary presence and his ability to be "an incomparable 'awakener' of men." He introduced a teaching that points the way to establishing an inner harmony among the thinking, feeling, and moving parts of oneself. Ultimately, one works to become the man or woman one was meant to be.

Cesareo often comments how Maslow and Gurdjieff complement one another. The former offers the proper theoretical model for psychological well being. The latter provides the practicum for achieving it.

"I had been thinking since the day we began the trip that I would like to meet some of the people who worked with Mr. Gurdjieff so that it might be possible to experientially know more about his teaching. Webster and I often read from the American translation of *Fragments d'un enseignement inconnu*, known in English as *In Search of the Miraculous*. It was Pentecost [the official celebration of the Holy Spirit in the Catholic Church]. I invited Webster to attend Mass with me at Notre Dame Cathedral. At the end of the ceremony after we had taken Holy Communion, I asked him to come along with me to visit Madame Jeanne de Salzmann (1889–1990), who had been Gurdjieff's closest student. After Gurdjieff's death in 1949, Madame de Salzmann had taken responsibility for the various Gurdjieff groups and institutes around the world. We had found her number in the telephone directory a few days earlier and called to see if she would meet with us."

At that time, Cesareo had asked for directions, explaining that they had just arrived in Paris, that she lived in a different *arrondissement* and that it would be helpful to know how to get there. "All the while we were traveling to her apartment I prayed silently. I wanted to be clean and pure the moment we met her. When we arrived at her address, we went to a corner café across the street and called her to tell her we had arrived. We spoke with her maidservant, who told us her apartment number, and that it was straight across from the elevator once we arrived on her floor.

"I knocked on her door. The young lady in a maidservant's uniform received us and told us, 'Sit, sit. She will come soon.' When I finished explaining to Mme de Salzmann what I wanted and why I had asked to see her, she told me to contact her son Michel. I recall so vividly what happened next. She rose from her chair and began to walk across the room to a desk, opened a drawer, and handed me her son's address and phone number written on a sheet of paper. She did all this in a manner I have never forgotten. She was perfectly attentive to every movement and nuance of what she was doing. The way she rose from the chair, the way she extended her hand to open the drawer, the manner in which she walked—to all of these she gave an astonishing intensity of attention. Those moments have proven to be unforgettable. They defined for me, in part, what it meant to be conscious."

Of Dr. Michel de Salzmann (1923–2001), Cesareo said, "He became my brother. Our exchanges were open, truthful and sincere. I attended his study groups which his wife Josée led with him." Michel had established a center for the Gurdjieff work in a village high in the Swiss Alps. Cesareo and Webster accompanied him there that summer.

Michel was an extraordinary man. A psychiatrist by profession, he had grown up at Gurdjieff's side. He described Gurdjieff as a man of exceptional character who "had a genius for using every circumstance of life as a means for helping his pupils feel the whole truth about themselves." Michel exuded a penetrating happiness and intelligence that invited the deepest and best parts of a person to relate to him. He had a wise sense of humor. He traveled the world regularly giving practical direction to the many groups who were studying and applying Gurdjieff's ideas.

Knowing Cesareo's love for theatre, Michel arranged for Cesareo to visit Peter Brook, the eminent British director of the Royal Shakespeare Company and the Royal Opera at Covent Garden. Mr. Brook was in the process of founding a theatre company at the *Mobilier National* in Paris. After meeting them, Mr. Brook welcomed Cesareo and Webster into his company.

But working with Peter Brook and his company was not to be. This time it was Webster's family that began to send signals for him to return. Cesareo states, "I decided to accompany him to the end, since he had decided to accompany me from the beginning." They returned aboard the S.S. *France* in late summer. Webster recalls disembarking in Manhattan "with a new, unaccountable estimate of the possibilities of everything existing." Cesareo disembarked with pneumonia, which he had contracted in England.

Webster was met by his parents at the port of Manhattan. A couple who had been part of the Cumbres staff awaited Cesareo. They brought him to Rockport, a seaside resort and artists' community on the northern coast of Massachusetts, where they were renting a house. After recovering from his bout of pneumonia, Cesareo found temporary work as a dishwasher in a restaurant and as an usher in one of the downtown Boston cinemas.

Shortly after, he took an apartment let by the Reverend and Mrs. Greenwood above their home on Main Street in the Five Corners neighborhood of Rockport. Reverend Greenwood had suffered a debilitating stroke, and Cesareo helped Mrs. Greenwood with his care. After the Reverend's death, Cesareo looked after Mrs. Greenwood. He would keep her company watching television or strolling the scenic shoreline with her as the waves tumbled in.

That holiday season Mrs. Greenwood thought it a pleasant diversion for her Cuban friend to attend a social gathering at the home of another friend. During the evening a woman began to have a severe anxiety attack and was showing symptoms of a breakdown. Cesareo sat down next to her. Applying psychotherapeutic and hypnotic techniques with which he was very familiar, he calmed her and brought her back to herself. Afterwards, a gentleman introduced himself to Cesareo as the director of psychiatry at Boston City Hospital. He had witnessed the episode and was impressed with Cesareo's success. He asked about his background and where he practiced. He knew of a teaching position that had opened at Salem State College and wondered if Cesareo might be interested.

He was. A Stoneham mental health clinic also wanted to hire him as a psychotherapist. However, he chose the offer from Salem State to teach. He preferred working with healthy people on a day-to-day basis. After all, that's what Cumbres was about.

Salem State in the early and mid seventies was growing. Many students were the first generation in their families to attend college. They came from the working class cities of Salem, Lynn, Malden, Everett, and Lawrence. They had jobs and were paying their way through school. It was a commuters' campus with little housing available to students. Cesareo remembered this advice of the Cuban psychotherapist of his youth: "If you would be great, then go to the mountains and teach the poor."

He taught the courses for which his work with Maslow had prepared him; in fact, they were the courses Maslow taught on motivation and personality and for which Cesareo had been teaching assistant. His students were electrified by his dramatic, theatrical style, by his unquenchable fire for life and his zest for the great psychologies. Students gathered around him after class in hallways, in the Commons (the undergraduate dining hall), and in his office; they audited his courses outside of the regular enrollment procedures.

Ellen Sheehan recalls: "His classes were unforgettable. They were living laboratories. Whenever you walked through the door, you learned to expect the unexpected. He was quite a challenge to our assumptions about life, psychology, and about ourselves. Whatever the particular content of the class might have been, for example theories of personality or transactional psychology, the focus was also on yourself and how you were relating to those around you. You were going to learn as much about yourself as you were about anyone else's theory. You might look at yourself and others through the lens of that theory.

"There were some classes where he would disappear into the background. The class would seem to run itself. Students broke into small groups, then came together to discuss or debate things. People would challenge each other's assumptions. Nothing was taken for granted. Things were questioned and probed. You really had to look at yourself as a model for whatever the theory was. How does this apply to me? It was always a learning experience, although sometimes uncomfortable. For anyone who sincerely wished to understand himself or herself, he became a valuable guide."

During his year at the University of Kansas, Cesareo had lived with a group of students in Scholarship Hall. They shared living expenses, prepared their meals and ate together. Over the course of the year they became good friends. Scholarship Hall offered a practical model for sharing living expenses for some of his most promising Salem

State students. It could be helpful not only for undergraduates, but also for friends who had just graduated and were beginning their professional lives.

So Cesareo suggested the possibility and left it to the students to make their choices. They had gotten to know one another very well in his classes. They had been reading many of the same books, including the works of Karen Horney, Albert Ellis, Milton Erickson, James Hillman, Maslow and other psychologists oriented toward leading healthy individuals to larger understandings, including two of Gurdjieff's leading interpreters, P. D. Ouspensky and Maurice Nicoll.

They found the idea of living together appealing and began to investigate possibilities. Eight young men and women rented a house on Linden Street, just four blocks from the Salem State campus. Then a group of four women took another house in Salem. Four men rented a home in nearby Marblehead. Two women shared another house in Salem. Choosing to live together was up to them and the houses were autonomous. Cesareo made the original suggestions, but that was pretty much the extent of his involvement. Because some students had no credit record, in some cases he vouched for them. He joined them for dinners at the houses from time to time. If there happened to be a crisis of some kind, he might offer a solution. Once in a while he suggested activities, such as attending the circus when it came to town, Broadway musicals, *Equus* (a live stage drama), a Mevlevi Dervish concert of dance at Harvard University, and a Doug Henning magic show at Salem State.

A number of the young men and women took ballet classes at a Marblehead school that was part of a recently founded ballet company. Some of the men studied Aikido, an Oriental art of self-defense. At his suggestion, some took piano lessons. On occasion all the men and women from the various houses, and members of reading groups who lived on their own, would meet for a dinner at someone's house.

Referring to his experience in the resistance during the revolution, Cesareo called the formation of the houses anarchic in the best sense: relationships between people are based more on essential human qualities that are naturally expressed when people live together without the interference of authoritarian powers.

Cesareo stated, "I let people find their places. No one was told to do anything. They found themselves in a totally new situation and responded to the needs of the moment from their best instincts." Sometimes Cesareo had a particular person in mind to be the leader of the house. In some cases, someone else took over the role. "I did what I could to set the proper conditions for a happy experience. People ended making their own choices, of course," he recalled.

The composition of the houses was a response to the human need for belonging and connection to one another. The houses were another example of how Cesareo brings people together naturally and instinctively. He says, "Togetherness is what I have strived to create for others since I was a teenager with my theatre company."

He always seems to be asking himself how one person connects with another: for example, how what someone is saying or doing relates to someone else's interests. T-groups and psychodrama are all about who is relating to whom and how, and what learnings are occurring. Being with others takes us out of our fantasies and inner convolutions and faces us with something more realistic—another person, their needs, their glory.

Living together produced friendships. There were Christmas trees to be decorated together and holidays spent with one another. One of the women at a house in Salem had Mondays off. Every Monday evening when the others returned from work, they found the living room redecorated. Then there was the call to a women's house from one of the young men at another house. He was in his kitchen wondering whether mushrooms can go bad. Perry McIntosh tells the story being awakened one morning by a neighbor's dog licking her face. He found his way through the always-open back door and upstairs into her room.

Eventually seven or eight people rented a house on Amory Street in Brookline that had a big room where fifty or sixty people could meet together. Cesareo had already formed a male chorus and some of the women were crafting a large theatrical curtain. Monday evening was established as a weekly chorus rehearsal in one room in the house on Amory Street, while the women met in an adjacent room to sew. He encouraged some of his students to produce and perform little plays based on the stories of Mullah Nasrudin, humorous teaching tales from the Sufi tradition.

Cesareo's organization of these groups was brilliant. He kept a sense of discovery and newness in the air, continually bringing each individual to a practical confrontation with himself. Most important, this was taking place in a group setting. Healthy, decent young people who were open, friendly and warmly accepting of one another comprised the living and study groups. They were bright, searching, and struggling to be in touch with themselves. They were bid to honestly discuss their inner responses to what they were reading together and to speak always in concrete personal terms. They found much to respect, perhaps even to admire, in one another. Lasting friendships were formed. Amory Street produced two marriages, Linden Street one. More would come.

Ultimately Cesareo wanted to form a nucleus of people who wished to work on themselves with him towards increased consciousness, awareness and aliveness. He understood very well that such a nucleus is formed by self-selection. All he could do was provide certain conditions. As he tells it, "They understood very well that there was nobody telling them what to do. If they wished to do this work, they did it, and that was their initiation, you might say. They learned that when they helped themselves, they helped their parents. They became more loving to them. Helping themselves, they helped their families, and everyone."

Michel de Salzmann invited Cesareo and his friends for week-long sessions in the Swiss Alps the next two summers. Carpentry, painting, and grounds work were done in an atmosphere of intense attention and sincere sensitivity to others. Michel's happiness was infectious, and a good laugh shared with the group was never distant. Cesareo organized these trips so that they would include weeks traveling in Europe. There were excursions to North Africa and Israel and trans-oceanic voyages.

Cesareo recounts, "I began to actualize a wish deep in my heart. The notion of having my own theatre and stage company had been inside me for so long that at the first opportunity it leapt to become manifested. I brought in these people in different ways, each one according to his own individuality. I had my aim. Some compliantly adapted to it. Others, like Rick Heath, who had met me as a result of Cumbres, went so far as to make my aim their own. I was looking for people who had abilities of all kinds needed by theatre, which included keeping the books, carpentry and painting. I was looking for musicians, seamstresses, dancers, singers, electricians, and salesmen."

By now some Cumbres alumni had reestablished contact with him and wanted to be part of a new enterprise. From time to time some of them would visit him at his apartment at Five Corners. They would walk down Main Street to Bearskin Neck, where they encountered the extraordinary vista of Rockport's picturesque harbor and beyond, to the ultimate reaches of the Atlantic. As talk of a performing ensemble progressed, and as others joined in the conversations, Cesareo became increasingly certain of two things: first, they would need to buy a theatre; and second, he would be directing a theatre company largely for the sake of others. These talks laid the foundation of what would become *Le Grand David and his own Spectacular Magic Company*—a stage ensemble residing in its own theatre.

"I tend to think inclusively," Cesareo recalled. "Theatre is the art of inclusion, of ensemble-building, of being other-directed while at the same time inner-directed. It was essential for me to have someone to talk with about building a theatre company."

On these walks to Bearskin Neck, Cesareo talked of the shows he loved so much in his Cuban youth. The most magical were the productions of Fu Manchu, the popular and congenial South American conjuror who headed a large stage magic company. His ornately decorated costumes, sets and curtains were permanently registered in the creases and folds of Cesareo's memory, beckoning him to recreate them in America.

Fu brought lots of humor to his shows, and always had comic foils. In this tradition of theatrical revues that Cesareo grew up with, the clowns were highly polished performers. They were usually musical virtuosos who were also master jugglers with great dexterity and wonderful "bags of tricks." He spoke about training a cadre of clowns.

Cesareo has a tremendous love for the art of stage magic. He enjoyed recalling scenes not only from Fu's productions, but also from other great touring magical caravans that flowered in the early part of the twentieth century. Their classical styles contrasted gentleness and lyrical choreography with suspenseful drama. In the end the magician and his company spread joy through the audience.

"I might wear more than fifty costumes," he confided. "The work is to weave a visual experience that dazzles the eye and delights the mind of the beholder. Whatever we do, we want to create a sense of enchantment that is the quintessence of the art of magic. But first, we need a theatre."

Chapter Eight: How Do You Explain?

With two or three Cumbres alumni, Cesareo looked for theatres that might be for sale, as well as buildings that could be transformed into a theatre. He remembers, "We were looking for places to do theatre, including puppetry. The favorite place for me at that time was a barn on Route 128 near Route 62 in Danvers. Yet, we never got any conclusion to the barn. We wanted to buy it and turn it into a theatre, but the price was too high for us at that moment.

"Then we considered renting a place and transforming it. At some hours, we would present puppet shows; at others, stage magic. A local mall was asking $75,000 annual rent for a retail space that could be converted into a theatre. But in this situation, the place is never ours. It is always rented subject to their conditions.

"There were months and months and months of searching. We looked at a couple of theaters in downtown Boston—old theatres. They were showing pornographic movies. It was most interesting to study them because of the type of people inside. One theatre for sale featured strip-tease. We saw a theatre in Lynn that was similar to the Cabot, but the neighborhood was a disaster. We looked at a theatre in Stoneham, Massachusetts. The Salem, Massachusetts, cinema had no stage. After month upon month of looking we discovered that the Cabot was going to be for sale. It was a pearl in a necklace of historic theatres owned by E.M. Lowe. He was willing to sell for $110,000 and we made the deal."

It is important to understand that this all came together because of individual relationships with Cesareo. Eighteen friends invested $10,000 each because he asked them to. Each did it because of his or her relationship with him. Cesareo recalls: "There were relationships between Rick—who became our painter—and me, Webster and me, Paul—who was an attorney and who wrote up our articles of incorporation—and me, Ray—who was a banker and became our treasurer—and me, and others.

"There was no group. There was me and you. Each one did his part to cooperate. I went to each and each did it for me, because of the way I explained it to them. Each one understood that it would be good for them, and good for everyone else. But it was not a group working with me. It was me working with people and knowing who to go to, who could I ask for $10,000. This was nothing to be taken lightly. I would not accept money they got from their parents. I required that they pay for it themselves, if they were going to pay."

Some had to work in a restaurant for months. Some had to borrow from a bank based on their own credit worthiness. For some people Cesareo put the money in himself. Each case was unique. He needed to know what was proper for the individual and often courageously acted on their behalf.

I was not a part of the negotiations with E.M. Lowe, and because these matters were best kept in confidence among the negotiators I felt a strong wish to be included and a little sad that I was not. On the day of the sale's closing, Cesareo asked me if he could borrow my dress overcoat to wear to the attorney's office. He told me that my coat was permeated with good business experience and honest wishes for his success. That remark lifted my spirit for many years to come. Every member of the magic company today can come up with similar examples of Cesareo's extraordinary consideration.

When Cesareo put together the purchase of the Cabot, he brought with him a group of about seventy people who were interested in some degree or other in joining his theatre company. However, forming a theatre company was perhaps not his ultimate aim. His intention seemed more to bring his group to a higher level of association, to greater understanding of one another and of themselves individually, to create conditions where destinies could be fulfilled. A well-functioning group is not built in a vacuum, Cesareo explained. It comes from personal relationships that are made by doing things together. He said, "You have to have a restaurant, a movie house or theatre, or a book store, or a place to sell clothes; you have to have a business. In other words, you have to have a task to undertake together—call it moving a boulder from one place to another, if you wish. You have to have relationships so that that people are willing to work with you. When they decide to stop, then they leave, and you'd better be careful the boulder does not fall and harm you.

"My goal may be in the Maslow tradition, that is to have a group consisting of self actualizers. If I tell you about my childhood, there is something in me that connects with beautiful places in people. Buber called this 'I-thou' relationships. This helps to understand my whole incredible adventure finding Maslow and ending at Brandeis. It is ultimately incredible, period. So, when I ask someone to undertake a project, it is possible that something wonderful might happen to them."

Cesareo says, "It's not that I am asking you to join a theatre ensemble, or to invite so-and-so to dinner, or to do this or to do that. It is that you wish to do it, because you understand there is something there that matches your wishes for life. To me, that is mysterious.

"I say sometimes to myself there might be a destiny, a something higher that guides me that is mysterious. The Hindus have words for these things. Karma is the thing that life gets you into. Life rolls you along with it. Dharma has to do with destiny and now we have to talk in religious language. Maslow writes so beautifully about these things, especially his discussion of higher values in *Toward A Psychology of Being*. This has to do with what he calls 'Being values.' These are an expression of one's essence.

"As to how the various houses and living arrangements, and eventually the Cabot Street Cinema Theatre came together, well, how do you explain that?" Cesareo continued. "You could say that I went to *Teatro la Caridad* hundreds of times as a small child, so many times that I began to think that it was mine, it was my own theatre. As a teenager I formed a company with my friends. You begin with individuals, and eventually there is a group.

"If you are asking, how did the *Le Grand David* magic company come into existence and endure for so many years, you can begin by explaining that I have been good with groups even as a child. You can say that the quality of the group depends on the quality of the individual. You can say that everything we do is always in the context of a group. But if others have not been able to explain these things completely, how can we?"

Teaching at Salem State coincided with the beginning of a new epoch in his life. It would be the only one which did not end with his being alone. Looking back over his life, the period that began with his year at Kansas may be said to end with the Bay of Pigs invasion in 1961, going underground, and his subsequent protection by the Colombian Embassy in Havana.

He was alone during his year teaching in Colombia, which ended with his entering the United States alone. His years at Brandeis ended with his work as a psychotherapist at Solomon Mental Health Center in Lowell, alone. Cumbres had left him with nothing.

But when he retired from Salem State twenty-four years later, he was not alone. On the contrary, he had a large family called *Le Grand David and his own Spectacular Magic Company.* Something had changed for him for good.

Interior of the Cabot St. Cinema Theatre.

Stage of the Cabot St. Cinema Theatre.

Marco as he first appeared.

Cesareo (left) and Bill Balkus opening doors at
the Cabot (1976).

Chapter Nine: Moving In

At the time of the purchase of the Cabot, how many of the dozens of people around Cesareo knew the depth of his passion for theatre, besides, perhaps, Webster? Rick recalls, "Few of us had any idea of the enormity of Cesareo's experience. We knew him as a dynamic teacher and engaging friend, but we had no idea of the theatrical blood coursing through his veins. Nor did we have any idea of what it meant to be uprooted, of what exile is, or what it is to have gone through a revolution. He never mentioned his training in psychology or psychotherapy. Several, like myself, threw ourselves into the adventure. We had an essential trust in his judgment and leadership."

Cesareo prepared for the purchase agreement for the theatre with extreme care. He hired one of Boston's master stage technicians to certify the structural integrity of the Cabot's stage house and grid. Would it be possible to fly the movie screen, thereby liberating the stage for performance? he asked Mr. Stewart, or "Stewart" as he preferred to be called. After its 1950s makeover, the Cabot's stage had been hidden behind a cinema screen nailed in place. The grid and backstage area lay dormant and neglected. Stewart attested to their structural integrity and security.

Cesareo's preparation in advance for the purchase included sending Webster and another company member to New York to meet in person with movie distributors to arrange for the opening weeks' schedule. It's all in the relationship, Cesareo advised them. Establish the relationship and everything will flow from there. The underlying notion was to be credible to them so that they would do business directly. In this way the new venture avoided working through middlemen.

A month or so prior to the purchase of the Cabot, he introduced the idea of publishing a newspaper that would announce the cinema's offerings. The publication would pay for itself through the sale of advertising. It created a need for writers, paste-up people, advertising sales, and people to distribute an initial printing of over ten thousand copies to thirty surrounding communities. Cesareo prepared Volume I Number 1 two weeks prior to the purchase of the theatre. For much of the next thirty years he would be the creative artist designing each page. The first issue was laid out in a company member's apartment using every flat surface available.

Rick recalls, "There seemed to be about twenty of us there. Cesareo was directing how the material publicizing our first film offerings would be laid out, page by page. The space was so cramped and there was so much jostling that he asked me to stand by the page containing the finished layout for *Lawrence of Arabia* until it was waxed down to the 'flat.' There was such a sense of urgency that I felt as if I were guarding it with my life." The material was delivered "camera-ready" to the printer, so that by opening day, Volume I Number 1 had been on the street for several days.

White Horse Productions purchased the theatre on August 10, 1976. The next morning Cesareo's circle of friends became scrubbers, cleaners, dusters and polishers working at the front of the house, orchestra, and balcony, to ready it for the reopening the following day. Over the next few months those with steady and agile hands who were comfortable working at the top of ladders and on sixty-foot-high scaffolding highlighted the Cabot's antique plaster reliefs with gold paint.

The Cabot is practically the length of a city block. Running along the front of the building are two storefront commercial spaces. Above these were professional offices—vacant, neglected, and in disarray. Cesareo was anxious to put this abandoned space to use. To him it seemed that two of the former offices had "Aunt Aurora" written all over them. They could be used to make costumes and curtains. In another he could see a rehearsal space for the barbershop chorus, and that would leave three rooms for carpentry and mechanical assemblies for a future stage show.

Later in August, dungaree-clad magic company members-to-be began to clean and decorate this area, which has its own entry from the street via a stairway to the second floor. This row of refashioned offices came to be known as the "Second Story." The crew rented a floor sander, donned goggles, and stripped the hardwood floors to prepare them for refinishing. They applied coat after coat of polyurethane to the newly lightened wood and ended with a glistening surface. The walls of each office were repainted, and the large 1920s-style windows reconditioned.

On opening night, August 12, patrons did their double-takes at the tuxedoed ushers and doormen, the fresh flowers on counter-tops, the aromatic coffee and tasty pastries in the mezzanine cafe, the player piano in the lobby, the squeaky-clean auditorium and shampooed carpets, and all the other touches of elegance. Within a short time, these same smiling and gracious ushers were caped in knee-length black polyester with red silk lining. The public was transported to a Radio City Music Hall atmosphere (trips to New York to tour it and see its shows were *de rigueur* for all the company). This was the elegant experience of theatre and cinema that Cesareo had grown up with at *Teatro la Caridad.*

Look what had happened practically overnight: perhaps without his friends knowing precisely how, Cesareo had established a public enterprise that was also preserving part of Beverly's historic heritage. In an era when neighboring communities were tearing down their vacant vaudeville and movie palaces, the Cabot was pulsing with life, attracting a distinguished movie audience that enjoyed the service of tuxedoed doormen and ushers and the pristine elegance of a vintage theatre.

The theatre company-in-the-making was publishing a newspaper, and attracting first-rate advertisers such as the region's banks, finer restaurants, and retailers. To top it all off, they were receiving rave notices from the North Shore and Boston press. Townspeople commented that September how pleasant it was to see the theatre's front doors wide open at nine in the morning. There was a breath of fresh air and new life afoot on Cabot Street.

Meanwhile Cesareo continued his full course load at Salem State College. His classes had waiting lists. Within a few semesters he would be adding graduate classes to his schedule. Webster and two other full time staff members operated the theatre during the day while he taught. Cesareo would appear after completing his teaching day to open the mail and direct the evening's work in the second story, where the trappings of a stage show were beginning to materialize.

Chapter Ten: Marco & Le Grand David

In choosing Webster's younger brother, David Bull, to be Le Grand David, Cesareo chose a young man whose loyalty and devotion to him have been steadfast. David met Cesareo for the very first time at Easter dinner at his family's home. Webster had invited his mentor to dine with his family shortly after they returned from Europe. As they sat at the table, Cesareo's opening question to David was, "Tell me, how do you like life?"

David recalls, "No one had ever asked me that question before." He wondered whether it was just Cesareo's idiosyncratic way of expressing himself, like how are you doing?

"It just struck me as very unusual," David says. "When I've reflected on it since, a couple of things have come to mind. One, he was finding out my basic disposition towards life. If I had answered, you know what, I really don't like life too much, or life's given me a raw deal and I'm not too happy with the way things are, it's possible that the conversation would have ended right then and there. I probably would never have seen Cesareo again.

"I think in general he is interested in being around people that are more or less positive in their approach to life, are upbeat and basically happy about how their lives are going.

"The other side of the same coin is your attitude towards life makes a huge difference in your approach to things, your creativity and your ability to deal with stressful situations, to get through difficulties and solve problems. He was interested in finding people that basically had a positive attitude towards life and had all of those facilities and abilities that associate with a positive attitude. Like attracts like, in that sense.

"What I remember answering is, I like life just fine. Life has been very good to me. I've always had food to eat and clothes on my back. I feel very lucky.

"I wouldn't say that was the right answer, but it certainly was an answer that fell within the parameters of a positive approach and expressed a certain gratitude. I'm very thankful for what life has given me. The great Biblical line that I love is, 'What I've feared most has come upon me.' You attract what you create in your world of the imagination and in your inner conversations. These get reflected in the outer world.

"Those are some reflections on Cesareo's question to me, which I remember to this day. I remember the scene. I remember where I was sitting. It was just a very memorable moment in my life."

After graduating from high school in 1974, David entered Franklin College in Lugano, Switzerland. He saw Cesareo on a return visit to the States, when the forty-two-year-old Salem State psychology professor was beginning to speak with his friends about forming a theatre company. He suggested that David go to the library and begin to research stage magic. "That sounded more interesting than going back to Lugano, Switzerland." David recalls.

Cesareo insisted that David complete his undergraduate studies, so the young magician-to-be applied to Boston area schools for the next semester and ended up matriculating at Boston University.

During the 1976 whirlwind of building apparatuses and midnight-to-four a.m. rehearsals preparing for the first show, David managed to complete his senior year and to graduate from BU with a major in psychology.

Cesareo: "David has a zeal for living, an inner spark of exuberance, an openness to learning and a wonderful sense of humor. He loves theatre. All these qualities plus his athleticism made him a natural—not only to play the role of magician, but to be a leader. Over the years he has demonstrated courage and ingenuity."

When Cesareo presented the idea of forming a stage magic company in 1976, it was David who leapt to it faster and further than anyone. His often invisible and anonymous hand is present in practically every ensemble project. Curtains and drops that hang in both shows, every magical apparatus that appears on stage, practically every set, all include David as a participant in their creation.

In an interview for *MAGIC* magazine, David recalled: "The clearest clues that magic would somehow be a part of this theatrical adventure were Cesareo's casual hints to me, going back to 1975, that I might find it interesting to study this or that form of legerdemain. It was usually very indirect. He'd say, 'David, I've always liked the one-man Floating Ball effect. Perhaps you can look into it and let me know what you discover.' Then, it was all up to me whether or not to pick up the ball and float with it, so to speak."

On Christmas Day 1976 Cesareo gathered a few of the men and some lumber in a room in the Second Story that had been used to prepare movie posters and lay out the newspaper. "Build it to last twenty years," Cesareo counseled. Strips of pine board were nailed together to form frames for canvas, which was stretched across the boards.

Then the canvas was prepared for painting by frothing it with a pasty liquid called gesso.

David continues: "Finally, on that Yuletide morning we began by building six seven-foot frames over which muslin was stretched, stapled, and wheat-pasted taut. A green, red, and woodgrain background was painted with festive Oriental highlights. Eventually, we would use the Appearance Screens to produce Cesareo on the golden top of a table at the beginning of his Linking Ring routine. While we worked, Cesareo kept up an almost uninterrupted stream of stories, filled with similes, cultural allusions, and jokes, mostly about the great traveling magic caravans he had seen while growing up in Cuba, the lessons he had learned forming his own young company before career studies, and how ultimately the revolution severed him irrevocably from those halcyon days."

The Sunday after Christmas, Cesareo announced to his group that he was forming a stage magic company. "Some of us are magicians," he stated. The door was open to any and all who wished to work with him.

Cesareo had been directing the preparation of the stage and grid area since the purchase of the theatre in August. A number of the men with a talent for mechanics and carpentry and no fear of heights had been straddling the girders of the grid. With vacuum cleaners they did away with fifty years of accumulated dust and grime. They installed pulleys, ropes, and pipes from which curtains and drops could be hung. The huge screen, which spanned the entire width and height of the proscenium and had been nailed to the floor of the stage for decades, was successfully rigged to fly. The Cabot stage was officially reborn December 8, 1976.

By then the "Golden Theatre Beautiful" sported two new gold curtains: the gold lamé contour curtain that rises vertically in scallops and the gold velvet traveler curtain that opens conventionally. Cesareo had asked Bill, a company member who was an architect, to build a scale model of the Cabot's stage house as soon as the theatre was purchased. This model was helpful in working out the logistics of designing and hanging these and other curtains. Forty years later, the model remains in our basement, thanks to Cesareo's insistence that it be preserved.

These beautiful curtains sewn by the women of the company first rose and parted for a short stage scenario on December 8, prior to the 5:00 pm showing of the scheduled film. A men's quartet sang a tune, and two company members who had diligently taught themselves to play piano performed a fiery duet arrangement of the overture to *Poets and Peasants* (an orchestral version would be the opening music for *Le Grand David's* premier). At the end of the little show the gold traveler curtain closed and the contour fell.

The Second Story lit up at dusk every evening in late December 1976. Around midnight some of us could be seen leaving, but not to go home to bed. We had a show to rehearse, and the stage became available only after the last movie ended next door at the Cabot. Into the early hours of the morning, night after night, week after week, month after month, table saws churned through lumber, sawdust gathered at our feet, finished illusions were carefully gathered from the room where they were hammered and nailed and carried into the painting room, where they were decorated. While all this went on—sometimes until three and four in the morning—next door, on the stage of the theatre, rehearsals were going on into the same very often not-so-wee hours.

The collective burst of energy which began Christmas Day 1976 continued for months after the first show in February 1977. Within fifteen weeks, fifteen new illusions were built, decorated, rehearsed and introduced into the show. New numbers required new costumes and choreography. One of the Second Story rooms became the wardrobe department, outfitted with commercial-grade sewing machines, where a team of women turned Cesareo's sketches into resplendent costumes, one after another, and where stories of Aunt Aurora's masterful creations became legend, so that one criterion of each new costume project was a single question: how would Aurora have done this?

Company members saw less and less of their pillows and more and more of each other. Cesareo was directing rehearsals until three and four and five in the morning, and then teaching a full course load during the day while other company members were at their "day jobs." A show was taking shape.

"Cesareo is passionate about creating beautiful things for the stage. He loves to do that," David says. Cesareo has said many times that without a vision of the whole, there can be no real direction. A good director sees what has gone before, what needs to be done now, and keeps an eye on the future. In terms of *Le Grand David,* that can mean five, ten and twenty years into the future.

Cesareo announced the opening with our own hand-made A-frame posters in the Cabot's lobbies. These featured placards that advertised the February premier to movie audiences. The first advertisement for the show appeared in the theatre's newspaper in January 1977. Cesareo often said that the show would succeed on the basis of attraction rather than promotion. Unlike large commercial productions, which often "mortgaged" their show in advance with a celebrity cast, his premier was paid for in advance. He and his friends had built the show with their own hands. They announced it to the public in a simple, straightforward manner. They painted the placards, and laid out and distributed their own newspaper.

Cesareo's descriptions used in the theatre newspaper in those days remain apt: "A wonder-making spectacle performed with joy and kindness in the colorful tradition of magic shows at the sunrise of the [twentieth] century;" "Entertainment in the Grand Theatrical Tradition;" "A full stage spectacle of Magic, Music, Comedy and Dance;" "If you are old enough to have seen some of these shows, it brings back glorious memories. If you are too young, it opens your eyes to a truly magical world."

Cesareo had chosen the stage name Marco the Magi, which is an English version of *Marco de los Magi* (the grammatical construction is the same as *Maria de los Angeles,* translated as Mary of the Angels). The Magi are, of course, *Los Tres Reyes Magos* of the Epiphany (celebrated January 6). Cesareo explains, "They bring dance, music, and joy to life, and that is magic." He sometimes commented that *magi* is plural because each of us is actually many. It is a mistake to think we are one and the same person always. To be human is to be plural. Cesareo's character Marco is many Marcos. Perhaps this is evident to anyone watching him on stage.

Cesareo wrote in a statement penned about a year later:

> On February 20, 1977, the Magic Company gave its opening performance. The 1-1/2-hour live show was preceded and followed by our regularly scheduled Sunday movies. Within two months, the show expanded to two (3 p.m. and 8:15p.m.) 2-1/4

-hour performances and the Sunday movies were eliminated. For two weeks in late July, the Magic Company was offered exclusively, with performances every evening at 8:15 and matinees on Saturday and Sunday. Again, for four days during Thanksgiving and during the holiday week between Christmas and New Year's, the live show was presented every evening with weekend matinees. Over 4,000 school children came by bus to see the show during seven special weekday morning performances offered over the first ten months. A series of highly favorable reviews in the local Metropolitan Boston newspapers, successful group sales, and enthusiastic word-of-mouth publicity are weekly pushing the 800-seat theatre closer and closer to sell-out capacity.

The cast grew—practically from show to show, and within a few months there were thirty and eventually sixty on stage. Those who had initially ushered or simply watched the show now had on-stage parts. In opening the show to so many, Cesareo was taking a risk. He was also creating conditions for people to find and develop their talents. He was strong enough to carry the show himself; yet he wanted others to learn how to carry it for themselves. He wanted an ensemble, a company whose members could play one another's parts, who understood the whole and could contribute intelligently to it. Cesareo's wish for the magic company, expressed earlier in his foundation of Cumbres, was to create a milieu where healthy, zestful people would work together to create something positively inspirational for themselves and their community.

On the other hand, bringing so many into the cast made him

vulnerable to the inevitable "Thanks, but we won't be here next year/ month/week, because . . ." The show would be completely adaptable to circumstances like these. The solution lay in Cesareo's flexibility and in the ensemble's ability to respond.

The Cabot's lobby became a learning space. Walking through the Cabot's doors required a proper work attitude from members of the company, whether they were there to usher or to work on costumes or carpentry. When you entered the theatre, it was to engage your best self in a specific task while keeping yourself alert to what might be needed. Anything short of that would justifiably attract a "wake-up call" from Cesareo. If barbs were necessary to move you to be more alert, he would toss them. Flowers could rain on you just as swiftly, accompanied by welcoming hugs and light-hearted jokes. He bid you to be honest with yourself. If you saw Cesareo's point, you experienced something that might lead you to a better state within. If you did not understand the way he was teaching, or how much he valued certain qualities within you that he was trying to awaken, then you tended to drift away. Everything was based on how much you valued what he was offering.

Wherever Cesareo happened to be, David Bull was usually close by, attentive to what might be needed and open to the quest. David recalls: "One afternoon a few of us were at the Liberty Tree Mall, where there are pushcarts and vendors in the middle of long, wide walkways through the storefronts. We discovered this vendor who had a number of colorful, finely made kimonos laid out on the floor in one of these long walkways. They were absolutely gorgeous. Coming onto this out of the blue was unforgettable because of what happened next. Cesareo spent quite a lot of time talking to the merchant establishing prices, and then he said, "I've got to go down to the bank to withdraw the money." It was obvious that this guy thought to himself that he was never going to see him again. We walked off.

"Cesareo withdrew a very substantial amount of cash from his personal savings and ten minutes later we were back. I think the vendor was shocked that this man had appeared, said this is what I'm going to do, and actually did it.

"This is exactly what the show needed. The kimonos were like manna from heaven. One of the amazing things about Cesareo is how he makes connections. If I had been at the mall by myself, for whatever reason, and I walked by the kimonos on the floor, I might have looked and thought, Oh those are nice, but not necessarily connected them with the show. I mean, we had no kimonos in the show at that time. He was constantly connecting things to the show. He saw them and saw the connection with the show. They are still on stage today, so beautiful."

That first show opened with Cesareo striking a large bronze cymbal (a gong given him by members of the company) hanging from its own steel stand that was placed in front of the stage. Although the opening sequence has changed over the years, the show has always begun with actors entering from the audience. To facilitate this movement, Cesareo had the stage extended beyond the proscenium before the end of the first year. At the center of the thrust, two three-foot-wide ramps descend towards the audience. On the sides, curved plateau steps create two more entrances to the stage from the audience allowing cast members to flow between the stage and the house more naturally and more often, adding depth to the show.

"Among my personal milestones during that first year was the successful introduction to the show of the three duck tricks," Cesareo recalls. "No other magician was doing them at this time. We were ahead of the times. It took a lot of work to build the two illusions from which the ducks appear out of nowhere and the third illusion, which is the vanish. Linking the three together was unique. Originally I was going to do them, but then I asked David to perform them.

"Choreographing a number is like painting a canvas. Its completion is the performance before an audience. You bring your ideas to people—the actors—make your suggestions, and let them take things in and see if they make them their own. Sometimes you have to think for them and tell them what to do. All the while you are fashioning something beautiful. And when it is finally performed before an audience, and you see the audience respond and the actors doing miraculous things, that is the moment of satisfaction. The painting is complete. You stand back, look at it, and see that it is good.

"There are many parts that make up the duck tricks. I began by suggesting the illusions to David and others who would help him build them. I asked them what they thought of this idea and whether they would like to investigate this particular illusion. Then they came back with questions and we discussed the issues of its construction. What's very important is how the illusions connect to what has gone before, which in this case is the Multiplying Bottles bafflement performed before a very unusual red and black curtain. The curtain was constructed so that it scallops upward from its center as a steward enters through it with the pieces from which David will assemble the first duck trick. The design of this curtain was so complex that I tied it myself to be sure that it was done right. Those ties have lasted thirty years. The first two illusions from which David produces the ducks are done to rousing music. Then what? Silence. The vanish is done to silence until the last moment when the audience gasps at their disappearance and the tumultuous rush of dramatic full orchestra underscores the movement into . . . what? How do you follow the final vanish? You have taken the audience's breath away with a grand slam in the bottom of the ninth, now what?

"The Rings. It has to be absolutely spectacular to follow the ducks. It begins portentously with the entrance of the ghosts brandishing swords. It turns into a big number, which it needs to be.

"The duck tricks are beautifully painted with colorful motifs on black lacquer. The costumes and sets reflect the colors of the apparatuses. Each of the three illusions requires exquisite timing. I directed them to give David the opportunity to joke with the audience as he is making the ducks comfortable before they vanish, and the comedy is practically all with his facial expressions. Every movement of the men assisting him during the vanish is measured. Even the bumbling misdirection of the clown. The unforgettable moment for me was the introduction of the tricks to the show after all the preparation. They got great applause, because the audience was truly flummoxed, but my satisfaction did not come from that. It came from the feeling of a job well done. I had undertaken the project, had known what I wanted it to be in the end, and had seen it through to completion."

Exactly one year after the December 8 inauguration of the Cabot stage, the very first host of one of the very first magazine shows for television, Marty Sender of WBZ-TV's *Evening Magazine,* aired a lengthy segment on "An extraordinary exhibition of stage magic," (Mr. Sender's description of the show whose name by then had become *Le Grand David and his own Spectacular Magic Company).*

The cameras captured Marco as he propelled himself several feet into the air above a horizontal illusion intended to enclose him (known as the Thin Saw), and then slithered in, so that only his head and feet showed. He would be sliced in two and then re-joined. The television audience got a taste of how, in illusion after illusion, he dazzled and thrilled. The show was designed for him to perform the most athletically demanding roles, that is, he was the one getting divided in two, appearing from boxes that had just been shown to be empty, disappearing from cabinets he had just gotten into, levitating in the air, and escaping from chains, stocks and other imprisonments. Because that role is most susceptible to injury, he assumed it rather than put anyone else at risk.

In 1978 Bob Lund (1925-1995), founder and curator of the American Museum of Magic in Marshall, Michigan, met Cesareo. He had heard about *Le Grand David* from his friend Dan Waldron and initiated a correspondence with Cesareo and company. Dan wrote recently, "[Bob] could detect the presence of love with an almost uncanny perceptiveness. To him, the practice and collecting of magic was a matter of love . . ." They met face to face in the summer of 1978 and formed an enduring friendship.

After seeing the show with his wife for the first time, Bob wrote Cesareo, "We thank you for one of the most wonderful adventures of our lives, visiting you in Beverly . . . we thank you for the privilege of seeing you perform—the grandeur and joy of it all. My head is still spinning. It will take me weeks to sort it out. It was one of the great adventures of my life."

Bob sorted it out very well. He believed that magicians who thought magic had something to do with confounding an audience with

113

tricks were missing the real secret of their trade. In a feature article for *Michigan History* in 1979, Bob wrote about what makes Marco and his troupe so fine. "Conjuring, to use a better word than magic, is the art of creating a sense of enchantment, of make believe, of the wonder-of-it-all in the human mind." He went on to write that "Marco has put on the finest magic show in the world today" because, among other things, his show is testimony to "the real magic [of] reaching the imagination of the beholders."

"Cesareo is *sui generis*. He has accomplished something unique in the history of conjuring. The eagle has never flown so high; never a magic show like this and probably never again if and when the company Cesareo has assembled is disbanded, perish the day," Bob wrote the next year for the British journal of magic, *Abracadabra*. In this article he spelled out just why *Le Grand David and his own Spectacular Magic Company* is the finest in the world.

"There is a camaraderie among them, a sense of family, and they appear to have a genuine concern for each other," he wrote. He quoted Cesareo: "The real magic of this company is that so many people have worked so long in harmony . . . simply for the love of it."

"There is also a concern for the audience," Bob noted. "It is expressed in so subtle a way that you are not aware of it until later, after the show is over and you reflect on it. All the illusions that might be frightening to children have been tempered in some way so the audience understands there is no cruelty involved. The element of mystery remains—how is it done?—but the audience is not concerned that the performers have suffered indignity or harm."

Bob went on to write about the props, costumes and curtains. He noted that they are all magnificent and are made by the company members. He wrote, "All props, from the smallest box to the largest illusion, are decorated with flowers, dragons, fans and landscapes. Most of this is lost on the audience because of the distance from the seats to the stage. So why bother? 'We do it,' Cesareo explains, 'for our own enjoyment.'

"Finally," Bob notes, "there is the theatre where this most stunning magic show is performed. Constructed as a vaudeville and movie house in 1920, the theatre . . . is the most immaculate . . . I have ever been in." He describes the sparkle of its wonderful ambience, including fresh cut flowers all about: "a sign directing the audience to an area on the mezzanine where refreshments are sold during intermission is not printed or hand-lettered, as one might expect. It has been done in needlepoint by a seamstress."

For *Abracadabra* (Dec. 20, 1980), Bob concluded:

> There are several things wrong with all this and it cannot be.
>
> The United States has not had a resident magic company since the days of Heller, Hermann and Kellar and the world has not had a resident magic company since Maskelyne, Devant and Egyptian Hall. It will not work. It is doomed to fail. But it has worked and it hasn't failed. The company will soon put on its 500th performance.
>
> If you are foolish or daring enough to embark on such a venture, you do not locate it in Beverly, Massachusetts. You need a more metropolitan, more cosmopolitan setting—New York, Las Vegas, London, Paris, Tokyo. Beverly is the wrong setting

just as Colon and Bideford [homes of two of the world's leading manufacturers of magic illusions] are the wrong locations from which to conduct a magic manufacturing business, just as Alcester [England, where *Abracadabra* is published] is the wrong place to publish a weekly magic magazine. The audiences will never come to Beverly. But they do.

If you are determined to ignore those admonitions, you do not select as your leader-producer, director, choreographer, catalyst, patriarch a virtually unknown emigre from the academic world. Pelaez was born in Cuba and is a naturalized American. He teaches psychology at a college in Salem, nearby Beverly. He is the wrong man from the wrong background. The undertaking calls for someone with a vast practical experience in the theatre, backed up by the right financial connections, to carry it off. But Pelaez has carried it off and on a grand scale. Compounding all the errors he made, Pelaez surrounded himself with the wrong people. They are businessmen, housewives, students, architects, lawyers, insurance salesmen, teachers, engineers . . . undisciplined dreamers who know nothing of magic, nothing of the theatre. They are eager for the adventure, but they do not have the training or tools to climb the mountain. They will slip. They will fall. But they have not stumbled, they have scaled the highest peak.

On May 12, 1980, a two-page, six-color-photo feature article in *TIME* magazine brought Cesareo and company international recognition:

"With the crash of a gong, the curtain flies up and smoke billows out from the stage as a team of magicians begins 2-1/2 hours of joyous entertainment that recalls the most opulent days of vaudeville. . . . Spectacular it is. . . The real magic about *Le Grand David* is the cast and their locale. The show goes on not on Broadway but in Beverly, Mass., a Boston suburb, though it looks as lushly endowed as any Great White Way musical."

The following year a 2,500-word feature article with eight color photographs entitled "Illusions become reality for pals of Marco the Magi" appeared in *Smithsonian* (November 1981). Bob was thrilled by the recognition the company had garnered. His letter to the editor of *Smithsonian* (January 1982) expanded on the historical significance of Cesareo's achievement.

In 1983, Cesareo invited Bob to accompany him and the magic company to their second performance (of seven) at the White House. Seeing an audience of 30,000 children and adults on the White House lawn applauding Marco's stage production and eager for photographs with him and his beautifully costumed company gave Bob a new perspective on *Le Grand David*. In an article for *Genii* magazine he wrote, *"Le Grand David* is the first magic show to become a national institution in this country. Other magic shows . . . became American traditions. Audiences looked forward to seeing the shows year after year. But a tradition is not an institution. *Le Grand David* has attained the status of an institution. They are a credit to all of us and that counts for something." Later he wrote for *Abracadabra,* "Of all the practitioners of the presto trade in the U.S., none has better credentials to the title of America's national magic company than *Le Grand David"* and marveled that the company had attained such eminence while remaining anchored in a small New England town.

One of the most eloquent descriptions of Cesareo's performances came from the pen of John Fisher in a cover article for *The Magic Circular* in 2002:

As a performer, you can have all the dreams in the world and they will turn to dust if you lack one thing, namely talent. It helped that Cesareo had considerable talent. Indeed had his career taken a path that led directly to entertainment at its inception, Cesareo Pelaez would still have become one of the greatest magicians in the world.

He is a remarkable man, but he is no less considerable a performer, with an ability to cast a special spell over an audience the moment he makes his presence known onstage. Cesareo's relationship with the audience is unique. It is conspiratorial, conducted in almost whispered confidences in the manner of many of the great music hall comedians. There is no shouting, no bombast . . . His eyes twinkling, there is a hint of mischief in everything he says and does and, as with all the great stage masters, his special moments are those when the large props are put aside and the focus is placed upon the personality of the man.

Cesareo's trademark trick is possibly the simplest in the show, his Floating Table. He tells us of the impending miracle, his words betraying that essential link to common culture without which any popular entertainer is doomed: "It's incredible, it's unbelievable, it's far out!" When he attempts the trick and fails the people in the audience audibly sympathize. When he presents the trick for his own self-delusion—going down slowly on bended knee to create for himself the illusion of a table rising, they are in hysterics. When the table genuinely floats, they give him a standing ovation.

Phil Willmarth, president-elect of the International Brotherhood of Magicians and longtime editor of their official magazine, said of Cesareo, "He shares his humanity with the audience in the Floating Table when he's down on his knees and he tells them, 'It gets harder every year of my life to get this table down.' That's true for all of us. And it's the wonderful thing about his character—he never loses his humanity. On the contrary, he is open about his failures and difficulties and always seems to be asking the audience for help."

Phil goes on, "This show gives a sense of total escape into a panorama of things that are happening on stage done enthusiastically, with joy, for fun, and you can't help but be uplifted by that experience. I think that is the basic reason for the success of the show. You are just inundated with a spectacle of good feeling washing out at you from the stage. So, if you're a grump coming in, you are a happy person going out. I don't see how you can help it. If you ask me, that's very therapeutic. Cesareo has such wonderful contact with the audience. He really is an excellent showman—it's amazing.

"His facial expressions say, 'I'm so sorry I'm fooling you so badly. I'm sorry you're wrong, the queen is over here, I'm so upset about that.' He is a master at playing with the audience—teasing them gently, leading them along, then shyly admitting it—all really without words."

Hand-painted cover of
MAGIC magazine.

Le Grand David.

Ellen Sheehan playing
Mademoiselle Sonya.

Le Grand David.

Marco

The finale at the Cabot.

Le Grand David

A poster for Le Grand David at the Cabot.

Chapter Eleven: The Larcom

As the company entered its eighth year in 1984, Cesareo organized the purchase of Beverly's other standing antique playhouse, the Larcom Theatre, four blocks away from the Cabot on Wallis Street, thirty yards off Cabot Street. Built in 1912 on the site of the birthplace of Lucy Larcom (1824-1893), one of nineteenth-century New England's great poets and educators, it was originally managed by the Ware Brothers, who would go on to build the Ware Theatre (now the Cabot) in 1920. The Larcom had been renamed the "Fine Arts" in the mid-twentieth century when it was still showing fine Hollywood fare. Its marquee had now become associated with ignominious films. Whether or not the public chose to ignore it, the "Fine Arts" was a triple-X-rated cinema, smack within fifty yards of Beverly City Hall.

Cesareo had wanted the Larcom for years. If nothing else, owning the Larcom protected the success of the Cabot from imitators. Cesareo went to members of the company to ask them whether they wished to contribute to the purchase of the Larcom. For this purpose he formed "Abracadabra Theatre Associates" as a limited partnership. Contributions would constitute a commensurate ownership share. A significantly smaller structure than the Cabot with no land other than that on which it stood and attached on one side to a building that was in decay itself, the Larcom sold for more than twice the price of the Cabot eight years before, because the Massachusetts real estate market was at the beginning of a period of steep appreciation spanning the 1980s. Almost two dozen members of the company wrote checks, with Cesareo making the largest investment out of his own pocket. He also purchased partnership shares for some members of the company who could not afford to contribute. White Horse Productions was the general (managing) partner.

Some members of the company chose not to invest. As with the incorporation of White Horse Productions eight years earlier, it did not make any difference to the company as a whole. Members did not know who was "in" and who was not. These matters were kept strictly private. But what they did know was that, like the Cabot investment procedure, the purchase of shares entitled the investor to nothing. Cesareo made it clear that the investment was a financial effort made for the sake of the whole, for the benefit of the group and its larger aim. There was a purity required by this effort that forbade adulterating it with interest in financial gain. When some of the investors in the Cabot decided to leave over the years, they received their initial investment back and not a penny more. Even in dissolving their ties with the company, they respected the original intention of the investment.

Cesareo closed the Larcom immediately upon its purchase and hired a company to remove the notorious marquee. All of the projection equipment was also removed, including the screen. With these actions, straightforward and irreversible, Cesareo notified any and all that the "Fine Arts" was gone—period. What stood was the Larcom ready for rebirth. A year and a half of cooperative labor by the magic company lay between the day of its purchase and its first preview performance of "A Work in Progress."

Yet he was careful not to overwhelm the company with work. He hired professional upholsterers to outfit the orchestra seats with beautiful floral fabric, and he contracted with roofers, plumbers, and electricians. He closed the men's room located in the basement below the lobby and had new rest rooms built in the lobby. The outdated electrical system was replaced by up-to-code wiring suitable for heavy duty stage lighting. Professional carpenters extended the stage.

For a week Rick and a crew of painters worked fifty feet in the air on scaffolding and a rented hydraulic lift to highlight in gold the pressed tin raised patterns of the proscenium and front of the balcony. A new boiler was installed. The original silk wallcoverings were carefully repaired. The proscenium electrical sockets were readied once again for bulbs. When the Larcom first opened in 1912, it touted a new-fangled convenience—it was "all electric." As if to show its stuff, the perimeter of the proscenium had been illuminated with seven dozen bulbs. Now, after so many years, the bulbs would shine again.

Purchasing the Larcom was a triumph for the company, both in how they saw themselves, but also in how the community saw them. "Was there nothing these people can not do," was a common reaction from the public. But it was also a period of difficulty and, as Cesareo said, "the greatest difficulty is always people." One of those was a Salem State administrator who required that now, of all times, Cesareo increase his hours on campus. Some company members placed in charge of the contractors did not consult sufficiently with Cesareo. As a result, there were a number of construction mistakes for which Cesareo had to create work-arounds, with surprising results that made his staging of some illusions unique in the world.

"There were many times when artists painted something wrong," Cesareo recalls. "We had to go back and redo it. It may have been because someone failed to follow my directions, or it may have been an occasion when I intentionally left something entirely in their hands and their thinking was flawed."

Of Rick, Cesareo says, "He was able to cooperate when I made things very difficult. He came like a savior, and has always been very gently supportive and loving, difficulties notwithstanding."

On many painting projects, Cesareo gave him explicit detailed directions of what to paint. For example, the original painting of the Larcom's front curtain from 1912 was stained and spoiled beyond recognition. However, there were certain things in the design that could be saved, such as the tassels, which had been very well done back at the beginning of the last century. Based on this, Cesareo brought Rick a specific design for him to follow in restoring the curtain.

Rick's work was only beginning with this curtain. A dozen more would follow, including legs for the exits and banners across the top of the stage. Surveying Rick's work twenty years later, Cesareo told him, "Everywhere I look I see the drops of my sweat, but in the process you have learned to become an extraordinary painter."

Cesareo further commented, "At the beginning a group did not exist. There were several motivated and skilled company members who worked at the restoration. But, again, it was me and Rick, me and David, me and whoever. Yet, I knew when to be present, and when to take myself out of the way. Sometimes it took a moment of inspiration to make the right decision. Suddenly a whole begins to emerge, larger than the sum of its parts, a community of its own."

With that whole, Cesareo created an entirely new show for the Larcom, based in part on the feel of the theatre itself, which is smaller and more intimate than the Cabot. The show was paced more expansively. The style was even more old-fashioned than the Cabot—

Cesareo called it a 1912-style production, in contrast to the bolder and brassier 19(roaring)20s Cabot show. The Larcom show affords the actors more opportunities for improvisation and for surprising one another. David characterizes the difference this way: "There seems to be more time between the beats at the Larcom. I think of music. At the Cabot, there are a lot of notes in each bar. It's go go go. That's not to say there aren't contrasts, like the silence of the third duck trick after all that drama. But in the Larcom show there are perhaps fewer notes in each bar, that is, the notes are held longer. There seems to be more time for the characters to interact on stage, for greeting one another, for applause. People are transported to a different time, a wholly organic world of its own that appears before their eyes."

David became perhaps the only magician in the world performing Harbin's "Upside Down Production Box," which he built for the new show. David recalls that the odyssey began on his thirty-first birthday with a casual suggestion from Cesareo that he might like to build the illusion. Other passing suggestions from Cesareo have led David to new horizons, perhaps the most dramatic example being when he willingly accepted Cesareo's apparently offhand invitation to research some stage magic at the library. That was in 1974, before Cesareo began to speak about any type of magical production.

Robert Harbin (1908-1978) is among the geniuses in the history of twentieth-century magic. A consummate British performer, he invented a number of illusions which have since become classics. However, he seems to have kept the secrets of his "Upside Down Production Box" pretty much to himself. David describes the effect: "From a space no bigger than a bread box, Harbin would produce two tables, a large die, a fish bowl, a spring snake, and half-a-dozen thirty-six-inch square silk foulards, and end with the appearance of a stack of fish bowls!"

This ingenious illusion had been the closing number in Harbin's stage and cabaret acts. He was heartbroken when vandals broke into his van and stole this priceless apparatus one night during an engagement in Blackpool, England. He never built another, and no other magician seems to have had the moxy to attempt it.

David discovered that Harbin had in fact published the plans for the illusion—however with twists, the most notable being that they were not complete. Although everything may have appeared to be in the schema, it was not sufficient to build the illusion.

It turns out that Harbin had constructed his masterpiece with the assistance of one of England's foremost illusion builders, Eric Lewis (1908-1993). Mr. Lewis was a friend of Cesareo and David. He had spent two weeks with the company three years previously and had published an extensive account of his visit in successive issues of *Abracadabra*. Mr. Lewis explained in his correspondence that Harbin didn't always give away the whole enchilada; he sometimes held back major details or modifications that don't appear in his illusion plans.

David wrote, "In snuffling around the local Woolworth's and other department stores for articles Harbin describes in his illusion plans, it quickly become apparent that not all the things that could be easily picked up at the store in late 1940s England were not hot consumer items in 1980s America. I'm sorry to report that many varieties of biscuit tins, by that time, had fallen out of fashion. And yet, there were, and are, many other materials like epoxy glues and fiberglass sheeting that are lighter, stronger and thinner than anything available sixty years ago—things Harbin and inventor-builders like Okito could only dream of."

The project became on object lesson in one of Cesareo's favorite maxims regarding theatre operation, "Remember the whole." David continues: "He urges us to see things as connected and affecting everything else. Well, for me the Harbin Box is the perfect metaphor in microcosm of this suggestion. Everything in the box is related. If anything is lengthened or shortened by a quarter of an inch, all the dimensions change. The whole picture of how it all fit together had to be kept in mind; the aim being to make a seemingly impossible amount of large items appear from the smallest space possible. This taking place while the box is held upside-down with its lid open towards the floor." So many surprises appear from the Harbin Box that it takes the combined efforts of the comics Li'l Av and Albert Ping Pong to assist David in this illusion.

The Larcom show features David's brilliance and evolution as a performer. In his new dove appearance number for the Larcom show, David began by appearing four birds—one at a time—and then put them in a cage with Mademoiselle Sonia (Ellen) assisting. Then the cage with the birds vanished! David began to experiment with all the possible ways of appearing doves and fell in love with them all. "I wanted to show the audience every conceivable combination of dove appearances that exist," he said. "Over time I realized that really wasn't necessary. As with the billiard balls [one of his solos in the Cabot show], there comes a point of diminishing returns as far as the impact on the audience. For example, I appear eight billiard balls. If I start appearing a ninth ball and a tenth ball—well, I've seen magicians literally end up with arms full of balls, and step forward for their bow. By then some members of the audience may be thinking, enough already, enough of the balls. You got anything else to show me but your balls?"

After considerable reflection, David eventually took out the fourth dove. Instead, he added effects in the middle of the routine, like the serpentine silk, which he ties into a knot and watches as it unties itself. "Now I appear three doves, and they vanish in the cage and that's plenty," David says. "Its a nice example of the leisurely pace of the Larcom show, because it gives me more time not only to interact with Mademoiselle Sonia, but also to interact the birds. For me, the most important thing, besides the magic, is to let the audiences know that I love these white winged beauties." As each one appears, he break outs into a huge smile.

David was also ready with a sleight-of-hand coin routine known as The Miser's Dream or Minting Coins From the Air—it has several names. In discussing various possibilities for the show, David let Cesareo know this was something he wanted to work at. He investigated possibilities, experimented with some of them, and practiced. In the end, he told Cesareo what he had come up with, and Cesareo fashioned a whole scene out of it.

Cesareo enhanced the solo with a half-dozen women in black and white elegant gowns, spike heels, and enormous sculpted hats. The clowns assist David in their formal best—black and white tuxedoes. The setting is an elegant soirée, and David fills the ladies' champagne glasses before he begins appearing coins from nowhere. He drops them into a white handkerchief, and then reveals the handkerchief empty. He goes on to baffle the audience with his production of coins from everywhere, until he finally takes the champagne bottle and transforms it into a fountain of silver ribbons.

These fascinating manipulations are performed to a trumpet and orchestra rendition of a classic Cuban bolero which segues into a moving orchestral work from a Spanish opera. The set is a grand fairy tale palace with serpents coiling around marble columns, reminiscent of a royal party setting in nineteenth-century Siam. Cesareo took an effect that most people associate with a single magician standing by himself on stage—or maybe even before the front curtain—and turned it into a full scale production number with lots of interaction among the characters, particularly with the clowns: Li'l Av who holds the tray with the bucket and the glasses, and Ping Pong, who capers about with the coins and props to spice the number with laughter.

To the first performance of the Larcom production, on June 4, 1985, Cesareo invited children and more children—busloads of schoolchildren. "The truest audiences are often children," he said with a smile after a rehearsal. "Listen to their silences. What draws their laughter? To what are they indifferent? Children are sincere and direct in their responses. They will tell us a lot." At that preview performance he told his audience, while controlling his tears, that this was the first time in twenty years that children had been in the Larcom Theatre. In his own private way, he had been working for this moment for years. He had wanted the Larcom's restoration to be a gift to the children of the community.

After the children's shows, while Cesareo and friends were fine-tuning their new theatre and show for opening night, a sampling of their apparatuses, costumes and posters were featured as part of an exhibit on the history of magic theatre at the Museum of Performing Arts at New York's Lincoln Center. Also featured was a large bronze sculpture of the Broom Suspension illusion, fashioned by David F. Bull (Le Grand David's father), a retired business executive who had a talent for drawing and a love for sculpting. Three casts of the 500-pound sculpture were made: one for the Cabot, one for the American Museum of Magic in Michigan, and one for Cesareo's good friend Ray Goulet who had an impressive collection of *Le Grand David* posters and artifacts on display in his Mini-Museum of Magic in Watertown, Massachusetts.

While restoring the Larcom, Cesareo oversaw, as usual, the day-to-day operations of the Cabot's film programs and the weekly performances on Sundays at the Cabot. Of course, he continued with his full teaching load at Salem State.

Between the purchase of the Larcom in 1984 and its premier performance in 1985, while he was creating the show, selecting and building illusions, designing sets, curtains and fifty new costumes, and directing rehearsals, Cesareo performed twice with the company at the White House at the invitation of the President and the First Lady; accepted the invitation of the Society of American Magicians' Parent Assembly to bring the entire company along with sets and backdrops to perform at New York City's Hunter College Theatre as the sole attraction for their annual *Salute to Magic* benefit gala; provided Lincoln Center with materials for the exhibit; and . . .

Chapter Twelve: Letters

In the summer of 1985, just after the series of Larcom preview performances, Cesareo was elected to the presidency of the Society of American Magicians. Founded in 1902, it is the oldest and one of the leading international organizations of magicians. The cover and feature articles of the August issue of *M-U-M,* its monthly magazine, introduced Cesareo as the new "Most Illustrious" and include "From the President," the first of twelve monthly letters to the membership. That issue also contained a review of the company's performance at Hunter College for the benefit of Parent Assembly #1 and noted the company's fourth consecutive year of White House performances. By the time President Ronald Reagan was followed by President George H. W. Bush, Cesareo and company would have responded to seven invitations to perform at the White House.

As president of the Society, Cesareo instituted a Life Membership program that placed the organization on firmer financial footing and provided for the Society's endowment fund. His "Letters from the President" offered a panoply of practical and helpful suggestions for broadening the horizons of the membership. For example, the first letter was a tribute to the "unknown magician"—a theme that "means something personal to a man who came penniless and full of hope to this country twenty-three years ago, and it is a theme that means something to all of us in the *Le Grand David Magic Company* who appeared seemingly out of nowhere a decade ago, unconnected, unheralded, unknown." The unknown magician could be the Iowa farmhand who entertains kids by pulling coins from the pigs' ears, the barkeep in Louisiana who passes the slow spells by baffling regulars with the 21-card trick, or, perhaps, the average member of a local magic club.

The article goes on to recall that wondrous attitude of the beginner in magic, that time, that age when

> we were all quite anonymous, when magic was something bigger than we were, something we would forever aspire to but probably never reach . . . can we—even those of us who make a living at magic's bounteous table—can we keep the spirit of the true amateur, which, if I've got my Latin right, means nothing more nor less than "lover." Being unknown, in spirit if not in fact, may finally encourage us to serve the art of magic, to give it a fraction of what is has given us, because we understand that we will pass, but it will endure . . . It seems to me that the unknown magician is a lot like the river pilot described by Mark Twain: "Your true pilot cares nothing about anything on earth but the river, and his pride in his occupation surpasses the pride of kings." Magic is our river. We do it, when we truly do it, for *love*.

The next letter develops this thought: "It has always seemed to me that only when a person shoulders his way past his limits (which are to a great extent self-imposed, and so imaginary) can he get a glimpse of his potential."

In each of the letters, the underlying theme is interwoven with news about the Society, praise for its leadership team, and light-hearted stories. For example, after touching on the article's main theme, it might ramble to a story about a recent meeting, give news of the Life

132

Membership program, perhaps illustrate a point with a story about Cesareo's magic company and then come back to the theme from another angle. As a result, they read like letters from a friend.

The new year 1986 begins with a column about the language of hypothesis as a medium for change. Cesareo suggests that the tool which both magicians and scientists use to transcend the obvious and reach for the extraordinary is the language of hypothesis: "Let's suppose for a moment . . . I invite you to imagine . . ."

According to the personal construct theory of George Kelly, one of his teachers at Brandeis, it is not necessary to invalidate a current hypothesis to test a new one. One continues to live as one has, while at the same time testing new ways, new attitudes, a new approach to something:

> The magician suggests, just for the fun of it, that there are ways of circumventing the laws of gravity and motion. "Suppose we regard a body as capable of levitation, or of effecting an instantaneous change of position and velocity." The magician offers an invitation to his viewer's imagination, and if he is a good magician, what we might call an honest magician, he will not claim that the new view of the world offered by his art is a fact. No, he merely says, "Entertain this possibility for a moment," and those who do are themselves entertained.

What does the language of hypothesis—of "let's suppose," of make-believe—do for us? It invites us to be more than we are. It stretches us. Then there are those who will say, "But I'm fine the way I am." That may be true, and at the same time there may be another way to see something, there may be an opportunity to expand understanding. Cesareo suggests that the language of hypothesis is, "Let's straddle the fence together and see *both* sides. Then we can decide for ourselves what's what." The language of hypothesis is the middle way.

He concludes with a poetic metaphor of how testing a hypothesis is like wearing a mask. "Masks," he writes, "are symbols of dissimulation, of hiding the real behind the false. Which is the real child, the one who demands trick or treat behind the Halloween mask (is he disguising himself or revealing himself?), or the one who must stand up in front of adults and say please and thank-you? Have you ever worn a mask, a real mask, and felt suddenly very free to be exactly as it pleases you?" This is how the language of hypothesis might free us. The hypothesis becomes a mask. On the one hand, if we follow it, we may advance into the land of our dreams (what if I were . . .). On the other hand, we can be whoever we wish while testing it. This is the underpinning of the magic company, which provides a practical atmosphere conducive to change.

Another presidential letter dwells on ideas developed by the American philosopher and scholar Jacob Needleman in a chapter on "Magic" in his book, *A Sense of the Cosmos.* Needleman writes about attention and misdirection—passive attention versus active attention. "I could never watch or perform a trick that was being done with serious overtones," Needleman recalls, "without feeling the sense of something new and strange like the signature of another world. At the same time, my amazement never dimmed concerning the ease and simplicity by which people, myself included, could be made to see something that did not happen or to not see something that was taking place right in front of them." In other words, while hocus pocus offered intimations of "another world," one for which his young heart yearned, it also pointed out some possible roadblocks on the way there. If he could be tricked into seeing what wasn't, then is it possible that the whole world is a mite different from what it seems?

All the while Cesareo is pursuing Needleman's exposition, he keeps in mind a young magician friend of his (perhaps as a metaphor for the importance of not only understanding these ideas, but also of the adult magician's responsibility to the next generation to interest young performers in developing their minds, expanding their understanding of what attention is and how it can be developed). Cesareo wonders, "Will my young friend feel himself urged to administer what Needleman claims is the necessary and only antidote to the human condition known as 'suggestibility:' the exercise of *active* attention in all the affairs of daily life?"

Cesareo invites the reader to entertain the hypothesis that "if attention is a key variable in the conjuring equation, then it is, in fact, the spectator and not the conjuror who creates the illusion. The magic originates in the audience, just as the taste of the cookie is in the child's mouth, not the cook's oven."

"Needleman's principal concern is not how illusions are created on stage [and how magicians can misdirect an audience's passive attention], but on how they are seen and lived every day," the president's letter continues. "He is what we might call a philosopher/magician; and perhaps that makes his every experience, his every field of endeavor, a springboard for self-inquiry."

These presidential messages actually recreate many of the lobby conversations Cesareo has had with his friends at the Cabot. Mixed with lots of humor and teasing, he keeps his chats open-ended, so that people have a chance to reflect about how things apply to themselves. They are encouraged to impartially observe themselves, in all their many aspects (a little bit at a time) in an inquiring manner. Such sincere, practical observation is a good antidote to the illusions we may have about ourselves and others.

The "Letter from the President" concludes, "According to Needleman, it is the role of philosophy to make us wonder, or rather to remind us to wonder. Wonder is our natural state. We lose it, almost every one of us, somewhere in the passage from childhood to adulthood. Philosophy is there to light our way back to it, if we only will take it up and walk with it." Shortly after this issue of *M-U-M* went out to its membership, Cesareo received a letter from Jacob Needleman expressing his pleasure in reading the "Letter from the President," and indicating his desire to someday see the *Le Grand David* production.

Later in the spring, Cesareo asks,

> Can we be fully cognizant of our shortcomings, yet still strive for the far horizon. . . On reflection, I would have to say that this double view of things has helped sustain me in our ten-year run with the *Le Grand David* show in Beverly. I mean, gosh, anything can become routine, and one thousand performances on a single stage—phew. After a while, it seems the only variety is the variety we create. Yet, to go out on that stage and to feel the calling of the magician once again, to make the effort to bring uplifting entertainment, lightening, if you will, the world's weight of sorrows by an ounce or two each Sunday . . . this, when I remember, can make it all seem worthwhile. And perhaps it is.

His final column describes, among other things, his gratitude that also is expressed in a poster he and Rick created in honor of the Society of American Magicians 58th national convention in Louisville, Kentucky, at which Cesareo would hand the presidential wand to his successor. He thanks the magic company for their support during the year, and he thanks the SAM leadership and membership for a wonderful year. "As I now slip behind the veil afforded by the words 'Past National President,' I will not soon forget how easy you made the limelight."

Cesareo was named both an Honorary Kentucky Colonel and Honorary Captain of the riverboat *Belle of Louisville* as the Society of American Magicians saluted his presidency at that convention. The magic company accompanied him to Louisville.

When WCVB-TV's (Channel 5, Boston) *Chronicle* interviewed him as part of a feature on the company in March 1985, he was asked what he finds most satisfying about being on stage in Beverly. Cesareo replied, "There is a satisfaction in the repetition of something that we can do well. It is in doing it well again that the issue of responsibility arises in life. The challenge is to do the best I can do again and again. We wake up in the morning and it's another day and here I'm going to do it at my best. I'm going to do it as if it's the last one, as if it's the first one, as if it's the only one, as if it is this day I have received in order to live it the best I can."

Two weeks after *Chronicle* aired, WBZ-TV's *Evening Magazine* host Steve Aveson broadcast "New England Profile: Cesareo the Magi." Mr. Aveson asked Cesareo, "How do you respond to someone when they ask you how it's done; is it just a trick?"

He answered, "I usually say, there are many ways to do it. It can be done this way, and that way, and this way and then there's this other way. And if that doesn't work, try another, and if it still does not work, then try yet another. You might find one way, and then another, then another. I want to bring to the attention of young people there are many ways to do it, many ways we can approximate doing something. There is not one way. The experience can offer a sense of relativity, how the truth can be approximated from very many different angles."

Was Cesareo encouraging the television audience to consider the possibility of thinking more relatively and less rigidly? Is he proposing that we entertain new ways of considering things, that we question our customary ways of taking things, that we invoke the spirit of search, of hypothesis, perhaps of self-questioning, of a rigorous pursuit of alternatives? He may be concerned with the trick to becoming more intelligent, more aware of the complexities of things, of fostering a greater receptivity to life's surprises, and developing an openness to a point of view we may have ignored or have been blind to.

Chapter Thirteen: Heart Mending

In 1992 Cesareo's health was declining. For quite a while he had been experiencing periodic heart discomfort. A grimace of pain would shoot across his face. He would often sit down in the lobby, bent over, attentive to the sudden twinge. Sometimes this came before a Sunday show, and you could see him sitting and treating it himself, perhaps by remaining very, very quiet. Those around him knew something serious was going on. Where others might call an ambulance, he dealt with the matter without panic or apparent fear of any kind. Nevertheless, there had been one occasion when members of the company called an ambulance for him. That was in the late spring of 1988, when he collapsed during a rehearsal at the Larcom. The cardio-pulmonary episode was resolved by the EMTs and hospitalization was not required.

As the New Year approached, his condition worsened. He was experiencing chronic weakness, fatigue, shortness of breath, and chest congestion. Yet he pushed himself through show after show, leaving no question in anyone's mind that he was pressing his limits. On weekdays after school he would go directly home instead of stopping at the theatre to check the mail and spend time with his friends. Nor would he be around in the evening, and this was unheard of. He was always around, or on his way, it seemed. Instead, he was now conserving his energy for teaching and performances.

After a Sunday show in late March 1993, Cesareo asked David to take him to Beverly Hospital, where he was immediately whisked off to the cardiac intensive care unit for the next two days. The diagnosis was congestive heart failure and cardiac arrhythmia.

Cesareo remembers: "When I was in the hospital, the doctors told the nurses that I had performed the show Sunday afternoon while having a heart attack and that they did not expect me to live. Seven-year-old Martha [Katie and Webster's daughter] came to visit me. I don't know how she got in. I was in intensive care. There were no visitors allowed. She came to my bed and she told me not to worry, that everything would be OK."

The sixty-four-year-old Cesareo spared no time returning to the saddle, although he slowed his pace a bit. He left the hospital in a matter of days, but only two days later an ambulance rushed him back. He had stopped breathing. David saved his life with artificial respiration. Once again he managed a release within a few days, and was back on stage within a Sunday or two, doing his full tilt. It would not be for another five years, when he was significantly weakened by a bout with pneumonia, that his condition compelled him to acknowledge new physical limitations and to give away more of his strenuous stage roles. Nevertheless he kept doing the Linking Rings, which requires upper body strength and leaping onto and off of a three-and-a-half-foot-tall table top.

Cesareo's mealtimes were now seasoned with a panoply of pills. He sometimes observed that he was being kept alive by artificial means and credited his physician, Dr. Roy Ruff, with staving off the Grim Reaper. Dr. Ruff recognized that performance was vital to his well-being and directed his treatment accordingly.

Around this time, Cesareo decided to go ahead with the reconstruction of the building attached to the Larcom. Built in 1918, six years after the Larcom Theatre, 9 Wallis Street was purchased at the beginning of 1993, just three months before his hospitalization. He set to work transforming the building. Three years of construction later, the company ended with a practically new structure that features a Grand Salon; a set of galleries displaying a collection of the company's hand-made apparatuses, posters, paintings, and costumes; a dance rehearsal studio; a library and sitting room; an apartment for guests; and a caretaker's apartment.

Cesareo had wanted a private space for holiday meals and birthday parties. For almost twenty years he rented handsome facilities in a local inn for many of these occasions. But it was not the same as being in one's home. When it was completed in 1996, the Grand Salon became this home, in addition to serving as an extension to the small Larcom lobby. It is an elegant room with a marble and exotic hand-made wood parquet floor, rich oak woodwork (that extends throughout the building), mirrored and cut-glass walls, a full-service kitchen, and semi-circular oak concessions bar. It is lit by hundreds of inset ceiling flood lamps augmented by almost fifty hung stage floods. The initial impression is stunning.

After his second hospitalization, Cesareo began to pace himself and to be more sensitive to his health. Through the seventies and eighties he had been teaching full time during the days, adding graduate and continuing education courses in the evenings to earn extra money to help sustain the new theatrical venture. He lightened his course load after his hospitalization.

The Society of American Magicians' 67th annual convention met in Boston in July 1995. As in 1988, when a caravan of chartered motor coaches had brought 1,200 members of the International Brotherhood of Magicians on successive nights to Beverly from their 60th annual convention (held in Boston that year), delegates from the S.A.M. traveled to Beverly on two successive nights to enjoy the show.

At this Society of American Magicians convention, Cesareo received its highest award—Honorary Life Membership—and the prestigious "Illusionist of the Year - 1995" award from the Milbourne Christopher Foundation.

On December 31, 1995, two months after Bob Lund's death, Cesareo retired from Salem State College. At that time, Salem State president Nancy Harrington issued a proclamation stating, "Professor Pelaez always took pride in his teaching and contributed significantly to his students' learning. He will be enormously missed." That month Cesareo also received an official proclamation from the Massachusetts House of Representatives, which offered "its sincerest congratulations to Dr. Cesareo Pelaez in recognition of 24 years of outstanding, dedicated service as Associate Professor of Psychology at Salem State College." On June 14, 1996, Ms. Harrington informed him that the board of trustees had granted him emeritus status "in recognition of your fine quality of service to the college, your scholarly achievements, professional accomplishments and community activities."

After Cesareo's retirement, his friend Pat Markunas, a member of the psychology faculty, decided to bring his former associates and their families to see the Larcom show and to have a reception afterwards at which they would present him with gifts and good wishes. She said that they had hung a photo of Cesareo in the faculty lounge, next to pictures of Sigmund Freud and B.F. Skinner (who was once a visiting lecturer at Salem State). When Cesareo heard the story, he joked, "I hope I look good."

142

Cesareo came across an article in the *Beverly Citizen* in late summer 1996 announcing that a noted muralist would teach a class at Montserrat College of Art and that he would select a wall in downtown Beverly for the project. His name was Josh Winer. He had painted perhaps the most well known mural in Boston, the Newbury Street Mural, a painting five stories tall and fifty feet wide that includes portraits of more than fifty famous Bostonians. The chairman of the department of painting at Montserrat stated, "Every artist has seen that mural he did on Newbury Street and it establishes that street as the art center of Boston." Various civic leaders were speculating about what the Beverly mural's theme would be and where it would be painted. "It's an exciting possibility," opined the mayor.

One sunny morning in early September, while walking down Cabot Street, Josh Winer and Cesareo met quite by accident. The results appeared in the September 18 issue of the *Beverly Citizen:* "A world-famous muralist has found a canvas in Beverly, on the side of the Cabot Street Cinema." Josh Winer says, "I'm very excited about the project. This is a good start to what I am sure will be a fun class. This is a way of putting the magic show out on the street. This is a way of taking what is inside the theatre and putting it outside." School officials confided that they received over three hundred requests from businesses within a thirty-mile radius, all offering their walls for the project.

Eye on the Town, presented on Continental Cablevision, chronicled the painting of the mural by the class. Mr. Winer explained on camera that he began by walking the downtown area with his class "to find a good site for a piece of public art, an outdoor mural. As soon as I saw this [wall of the Cabot Street Cinema Theatre] I thought, 'you can't get better than this.' The architectural features are interesting.

143

The more I learned about the company itself, *Le Grand David,* the more I realized that it was a rare opportunity to create a mural that celebrated something that's very, very unique."

Cesareo was closely involved in the design of the mural, and the *Eye on the Town* feature shows him offering his ideas to the class in an informal setting. The mural was painted over the course of several months in 1996. As Mr. Winer explains in the film, because of the proper preparation of the brick surface and the selection of special paints, the mural will last for the life of the building.

Chapter Fourteen: David, Martha, & Marian

David won the Christopher "Illusionist of the Year" award in 2000. Two years prior, a colorful photographic collage of him in action during both the Cabot and Larcom shows appeared on the cover of the June 1998 issue of *The Linking Ring*. The cover story by editor Phil Willmarth praises David as an "extremely talented and skillful magician."

One Sunday evening following a Cabot performance, Ellen e-mailed Cesareo this story:

> After the show, when you were praising David and his performance, I wanted to tell you this little story but just couldn't find the words at the time.
>
> Just before the Multiplying Bottles, Li'l Av was flipping his hat with his usual flair and it surprisingly bounced off his head to the stage floor (which of course is perfectly acceptable for a character with very big shoes and a red rubber nose, but our dear clown was chagrined because he always tries so hard to do his best). With a dance-like move, David gracefully picked up Av's hat, dusted it off, and gave it back to the grateful clown with a smile. In that moment of improvisation, with one gesture David showed an attentiveness, grace and kindness which beautifully expressed the nature of this company you have created.

Like Cesareo, David has had to rise above illness and injury. The magic world is not without its dangers. A few years ago David accidentally fell through an open service door in the floor backstage and injured his knee so severely that he was prevented from doing some illusions. Others had to fill in for him for several months. When asked about the accident he replied:

"Well, I remember the injury very clearly because it happened maybe two or three weeks before 9/11 in 2001. We were on our annual August vacation from performing and I was working backstage. There's a service door in the floor off stage left in the back corner of the stage. We use it to shuttle props up and down during the show.

"I was back there one day, and didn't take my own advice, which I give to people all the time: it doesn't matter if you think you're coming right back up, always close the lid behind you. I remember distinctly going through and leaving it open, leaving the hinged board that covers the opening in the up position, and thinking, I'm going to be coming right back up, so I don't need to close it. I'll save myself a few seconds." For whatever the reason, David crossed underneath the stage and went up the other side, thereby leaving the lid open.

"The next day I went back there to get something," David continued. "The lights were out but I go back there all the time with lights out. You navigate, because you're back there a thousand times and you know your way around. I didn't even have a flashlight with me. I was going to the bookshelves in the back where we store props. There's a light back there and I was going to turn it on. Of course, there's the lid left open in the dark. It was one of those moments when my foot goes in and starts to fall down and in that split of a second I know what happened and why it happened. It's like people talk

146

about reliving your life at the moment of your death. Well, this was like reliving all the chain of events that got me to that moment.

"So my right leg went straight down with nothing to break the fall and my left leg went out sideways—still out on the stage level—and my knee bent in a very bizarre position, in a way that knees are never supposed to bend. I knew immediately that I had done something that was serious. It hurt a lot. I remember lifting myself back up, because as I was falling I had spread my arms and caught myself on either side of the trap. By the time my shoulders were level with the stage, it was too late as far as the knee injury. Of course, the amazing thing is it could have been a lot worse. I could have hit my head and bled to death. I could have knocked my front teeth out. I could have done a lot of things, but the end result was the medial ligament on the inside of my left knee was hurt. I didn't know if was torn, if it was separated, but something serious had happened.

"I lifted myself up and sat on the side of the opening with my legs down and my knees dangling, my feet and calves swinging back and forth, trying to assess the damage. I was able to stand up. I was able to walk kind of dragging my left leg behind me."

It turned out to be an injury that, literally, time healed. By the time the season opened, David was able to get through the show with some help on physically demanding numbers. Week by week the knee got stronger.

David concluded, "It was just one of those things where the best thing is just leave the self-pity at the door. See what the injury is, see what you have to do to deal with it. You are not going to cancel shows because of it. The decision was made not to have an operation, so that wasn't an issue. It took about eight months before it felt normal. That was the early summer 2002. It was just one of those things that happens along the way. You keep your fingers crossed and you do what you have to do to keep on going."

David's nieces Martha and Marian grew up on stage with the magic company. They made their stage debuts while still toddlers and performed regularly through their early teens, when they went away to high school. Cesareo tells the story of how Marian chose Blacky:

"We went to New Hampshire to the lady with the litter of puppies. While we were speaking with her, Marian picked up a puppy and held her in her arms. The lady said, 'Oh no, not that one. Why, she's the runt of the litter. I can't sell her to you.'

"Marian just held the little puppy.

"The lady said, 'No, look at some of these over here. They're just fine.' So we did. But Marian did not budge. She lovingly held the puppy.

"The lady asked us if there was one we liked. We looked at Marian. The lady said to Marian, 'That one's not for sale. Why, her legs are not that strong, she's bound for difficulties. Why don't you look at her siblings?'

"Marian would have none of it. She loved the dog in her arms and looked content.

"Finally the lady admitted that the puppy had a hernia. We looked at Marian. She had made her choice.

"On the way home, holding her puppy in her lap, she named her Blacky. A couple of months later we painted a poster that featured portraits of everyone in the Larcom show cast. Marian was painted holding Blacky in her arms. She designated Uncle David as Blacky's caretaker."

When she returned from her high school junior year in Spain, Marian observed:

"My favorite moment in the show is right at the beginning, when I am standing downstage right and watching all the cast members on stage, just having made their entrances with their beautiful costumes, moving in such a pageant—everyone is there. I can feel their energy, I can hear the audience applauding and feel their appreciation. No matter how badly I was feeling before the show, no matter what my teenage dissatisfactions or worries, at that moment I begin to feel uplifted, and by the end of the show I am feeling elated. There is something about performing on stage which I just love, from my depths. I just love it. So the show is a medicine for me."

Her older sister Martha agrees: "For me as well, even if I come into it feeling physically sick with a bad cold or concerned that I'll have to make a dash offstage at any moment. But you know what, once the show begins, I forget all about it. And by the time it is over, I am feeling not only all better, but it's miraculous, I feel just wonderful."

Martha continues, "When I was very young I went over to Cesareo's house pretty much every afternoon. I'd swim in his pool and dive off the diving board, although water ballet was my favorite. I did a lot of water ballet. You know, Cesareo highly encouraged all of that sort of creativity in the pool. There was a general understanding that I could do whatever I wanted. He let me eat whatever I wanted, say what I wanted, do whatever I wanted, when I wanted. That was important in my learning to trust myself. Because nobody was there telling me that what I felt I should do was wrong, or bad, or whatever. I guess I was encouraged to go with my instinct more often—an important thing for me.

"If I were to summarize how Cesareo affected my childhood, one of the ways would have to be that I learned to trust my instincts. Of course, at the theatre, he really let me do what I wanted—like leading the dance [Saturday morning dance rehearsals for the women of the company].

"I was always treated—not necessarily as an adult, because I wasn't an adult—but treated with a level of respect, like I was an intelligent human being instead of like a kid. I was never 'a little twirp,'—that was really important. I know that in other situations outside the theatre, if people started treating me differently, speaking to me differently, because I was younger, it would really upset me, because I was so used to being treated as an equal by all these people at the theatre. And I can't talk down to children now. I think that's very much a product of the way I was treated by Cesareo and other members of the company.

"I was pretty much allowed to do what I wanted on stage. I started dance lessons at a young age. I was no Anna Pavlova at age four, yet I was given the liberty to improvise as I wanted. I remember during intermissions between movies, I would dance around the upstairs lobby while customers were there having a cup of tea. I was just twirling around in the lobby. I saw myself as an important source of entertainment for them. I was providing them with ballet before they saw the movie.

"Certainly part of me feels very comfortable on stage. That is very much a product of my being allowed to be creative and not being told where to be and what to do."

During the winter of her high school junior year in France, sixteen-year-old Martha wrote this letter to the magic company after a discussion in literature class:

All my dearest friends,

We were talking about family, and how it sometimes has a less fixed meaning than we often take it to mean in our culture. And all I can think of is you. I was raised by about thirty parents with about seven brothers and sisters. You are my family. No matter where I am in the world, I think of you all more than you can imagine. My friends here have all heard myriad stories about this mythic "magic company." They can't quite put their finger on what it is, but they know it must be something extraordinary. . . On rough days, the fact that such a place as the Cabot Street Cinema Theatre at 286 Cabot Street and that such unspeakably amazing and dedicated people get together every Sunday and create magic—real magic—is, truly, beyond any words. . . Magic posters envelop me on the walls around my bed when I sleep. You are all always with me—always.

Love,
Martha

Martha's first two years of college were at Brandeis University, about forty-five minutes from Beverly. Every Sunday she performed with the company, brimming with freshman stories. Her introductory psychology course happened to be taught by Dr. Ricardo Morant, the first associate Abraham Maslow had hired after he accepted his position at Brandeis in 1953, shortly after he had been given the liberty to create a psychology department at the fledgling university that was founded in 1948. Eventually he turned over the chairmanship of the department to Professor Morant, who had become a close friend.

Martha introduced herself to Dr. Morant, told him that she was a friend of Cesareo's, and asked whether he knew Cesareo. Dr. Morant of course remembered him and asked Martha to send Cesareo his warm and sincere greeting. Eventually, Martha invited her teacher to see a show. Dr. Morant accepted and arranged to bring several of his grandchildren, some of whom were visiting from Spain. He invited Martha and Cesareo to join his family for dinner after the show at his daughter's home in a nearby town.

Cesareo asked Martha to take a photograph of Dr. Morant before their reunion. Dr. Morant acceded, saying, "Oh, Cesareo may not remember my appearance, but I remember what he looks like!"

As the weeks passed, Cesareo and Rick secretly worked on a portrait based on Martha's photo. When Dr. Morant arrived for the show that December afternoon, Martha presented him with a finely-crafted velvet case. Inside were two silk-covered boards protecting the portrait. Later that winter, Martha invited Dr. Morant and his wife Paquita to join the company's twenty-eighth anniversary celebration in the Grand Salon. Dr. Morant observed that Maslow's work had found a true and practical fruition here, more so than anywhere else in the world that he knew of. He found it extraordinary that the company has been able to stay together for so long. "What you have here is a wonderful community. It is a testimony to uncommon leadership and enduring practical efforts," he said. He further commented that the museum of *Le Grand David* art and apparatuses is an example of brilliant forethought. "To know from the beginning that what you were doing here is of enormous importance to others and to future generations is pure vision. Cesareo really sees the big picture."

Poster: Marco, Le Grand
David and Blacky.

Hand-painted portrait of
Marian.

Ricardo Morant taught
Cesareo and, many years
later, Martha.

Hand-painted portrait of
Martha.

Wonderful Surprises:
Marco and Martha at the
Larcom.

Blacky in her puppy days.

The two sisters, Marian
and Martha, performing.

Marco, Marian and a
rabbit.

Chapter Fifteen: Luis

Starting in the 1990s, a few feature-length films made in Cuba were released in the States. Cesareo usually views films from his customary seat in the last row of the orchestra, where David and others often join him. These Cuban films he watched alone from a balcony seat. He watched them several times; subsequent viewings were often in the company of friends. Clearly it was a shock to see his native land again. He seemed to digest every image fully, again and again.

He kept his feelings to himself. Sometimes he talked briefly about the bloodshed he had witnessed as a young man. Conversations were more about the imagery of the films and the beauty and truth revealed by the auteur. Cesareo explained typical aspects of Cuba that appeared on screen.

His openness to things Cuban took everyone in the company by surprise. A man who, for as long as his friends had known him, had rarely mentioned his Cuban past, was now more at ease talking about his native island.

Out of the blue, on August 22, 2000, he received an e-mail. "Greetings from a resident of Santa Clara," it began. "Just some simple lines to say hello after some forty years since last time I saw you. I was a student of yours at the Santa Clara Marista school. I graduated with the class of 1959. Among my classmates were Guillermo Zapatero, Adolfo Ruiz Villaverde, Francisco Haya, Alfredo Gonzalez, Jesus Azan, and Enrique Machado. Do you remember those boys who now comb gray hair? I remember well the black VW that you had with your signature etched in gold on the doors. It was a gem of a car.

"Only a few days ago that I found out your whereabouts through another more recent friend who for twenty-seven years has been a physics professor at UCLA—Jorge Morales, PhD. He was two years behind me so he is younger but he was also your student."

The correspondent was Luis Puello, a name that Cesareo would probably never have remembered had it not been for this e-mail. Jorge Morales had accidentally come across an article entitled "A Magi named Cesareo" at the web site of *MAGIC* magazine and had immediately notified alumni of Santa Clara's Marista Academy that he had discovered their beloved English teacher (they knew him as "El Teacher").

Cesareo had just completed his twenty-fourth season at the Cabot and was about to leave for Sarasota, Florida, for a week's vacation. Now suddenly he was reminded of his stint as a lay teacher at the Marista Academy headed by Brother Mauro Lopez forty-five years ago. The students at that time were ten, eleven, and twelve years old. He recalled only one, and that memory touched him. That was the boy who needed kindness the most because he had real difficulties at home. His was the only name he remembered, but on the plane to Sarasota the stories kept coming back, including how he used to help the students put on their shows at graduation time. He recalled that Brother Mauro's teaching and guidance were so effective that it enabled Cesareo's asthma to heal. Flying to Sarasota, he began to see how some of the ideas that he used to teach in the fifties were still alive in the magic company after so many years.

"As soon as I got to Sarasota the first thing I did was to call Luis on the telephone and tell him this was Cesareo calling. He was so happy. He began to talk and talk and talk and talk. He wanted to tell me all of forty years in five minutes. And I couldn't take it all in. It was too fast, too Cuban. I said, 'Luis, I haven't spoken Cuban in many years. Slow down, please.'"

After Cesareo returned from his Florida vacation and completed rehearsals for the new season opening in September, he invited Luis to fly to Beverly with his wife to see both the Cabot and Larcom shows and to celebrate Cesareo's sixty-seventh birthday in October. In declining the invitation, Luis reluctantly informed his new friend that he was receiving intensive chemotherapy to combat an aggressive type of lymphoma. Travel to Boston was impossible at that time. He e-mailed,

> I'm still working and I'm not afraid anymore. My family has provided immeasurable support, and I settled my accounts with the Lord; this has relieved me of all anxiety. I am completely at ease, and have a very strong conviction that this situation will be overcome.
>
> I apologize for not mentioning this earlier, please forgive me. But I felt that it was unnecessary, and it could cloud the waters while we were getting re-acquainted after forty years.
>
> If your offer would stand for a later time, perhaps in December or in the spring, my wife Rosita and I would love to take you up on it . . .
>
> GRACIAS MIL POR LA INVITACION, CESAREO, QUEREMOS IR A BEVERLY. UN FUERTE ABRAZO"

Cesareo responded,

> I am a man of FAITH. You come NOW, come LATER, come whenever your heart brings you both to Beverly. The invitation is open. You and Rosita tell me when. See, the world needs a little bit of MAGIC.
>
> Tonight I cried and am going to bed praying for your prompt visit. May we all be blessed.
>
> Love to you and Rosita, from afar. You are also a man of FAITH.

On Cesareo's birthday (October 16), he wrote Luis:

> Yes, your greeting card arrived on time. It is exquisitely designed. It impressed me tremendously, and this is not a Cuban exaggeration but a fact. I have already composed six or seven replies in my mind. All of them unsatisfactory, short of how much and deeply I appreciate your gesture.
>
> For many years, close to forty since I left Cuba, I have kept quiet inside my memories of the *Collegio Maristas.* I did not have anyone to share, to speak to, to explain, to comment, someone who would understand what I was talking about. [Going into exile and coming to the United States] was like shifting my whole world, not only by letting go of Spanish but by placing my old memories in a safe deposit box in my inner life.
>
> See, Luis, the whole experience of *Le Grand David and his own Spectacular Magic Company* and the theatres in Beverly and the teaching at the state

college has been nothing but a restructuring of my identity, totally necessary for my survival. And in the midst of all this triumph and glory of identity there appears an e-mail from Florida, from a Luis Puello I could not remember. As if I have closed an airtight or soundproof door. Now yours and Rosita's communications, photographs, memories are very dearly appreciated by me. The doors of awareness open up, reflecting the depth and aliveness of my inner life; a whole world that has been put to sleep, but suddenly becomes accessible to conscious experience thanks to your kindness and goodness. So here goes my gratitude for all the good you offer with your friendship. I assure you that, although this time I will not be able to join you at the special alumni gathering in Miami, I will make arrangements so that at the first future opportunity that such a gathering occurs again, I will come and join you and Rosita for the occasion and even bring my Linking Rings to perform for all of you. This time I already have performances scheduled and promises to keep. So, I would like to take a rain check, if that is all right with you both.

Meanwhile, be sure that everyone here is waiting for your visit, and we would like to have you come as soon as possible.

Thank you, thank you, thank you, Luis.

Gracias mil . . ."

Cesareo continued a stream of positive healing suggestions and good humor through his e-mails and conversations. In honor of Luis's birthday in December, he arranged for the barbershop chorus to sing him one of the magic company's original birthday songs over the lobby telephone. Luis responded in an e-mail that day, "And among the well-synchronized voices of the whole LGD company, I could distinctly recognize one particular voice. It had somewhat of a Spanish flavor to it, and I remembered hearing it many years before when, full of foresight, it would say to us: 'pay attention now, English will be important to you someday, you'll see.' And now this voice, and the others, truly conveyed friendship, and companionship, and caring."

In an unpublished reflection on his new friendship, Cesareo wrote:

Magic, in all this, is in the relationship. The true secret of magic is the relationship. Peter Brook, the distinguished director, talks about the magic of relationship in the recent book, *Between Two Silences.* He says that over the years [when he was directing movies] he had come to realize that he and his actors were not making motion pictures. No, in fact, he states, "We're making relationships." He continues, "But we can't *make* relationships; we can *let* relationships, because that's what any story, any play of any description, anything human, is about: relationships. In scratching away to find the bedrocks of that, you're doing something like a painter or sculptor who is eliminating what's not necessary until the shape is there. That shape then becomes aesthetically pleasing, and I think that is what touches you.

It was obvious that all of Luis's great qualities when he was ten, eleven years old had begun to emerge: a wonderful sense of humor, incredible intelligence, and a great ability to take life responsibly. When he told me of his condition, I did not change my tone too much. I just began to be concerned and to care for him. And bring a little bit more humor to our relationship. We are looking forward to meeting him now. I'm sure the rain check is going to materialize soon.

Luis sent me the photo of *El Teatro de la Caridad* in Santa Clara, where the legendary magician Fu Manchu performed. To think there are so many Cubans in exile who were influenced by Fu and his magic. Fu Manchu was the idol of all the youngsters in the 1950s.

Luis also sent me his class photo. And contemporary photos of him, his wife, his baby grandson. He wanted me to see him without any hair. It's amazing in the photograph to see the awakefulness—and depth of the wisdom—in the eyes. Sometimes I feel that now he is the teacher and I am the student.

In March Cesareo e-mailed with typical good humor,

See, Luis, while you will be staying here, you are a member of this magic company, and I am the boss. And my aim is that you have the most wonderful experience of your life. I know that you are a good boss, too. You always were bossy. But in this case you have to give me the privilege of leading the circumstances.

161

Now, I want to wait until all the snow is gone. I would like you and Rosita to stay for a sufficiently long time. Don't give me American style protocol. We are Cuban friends. *Amigos.* There are over forty years of talk to be had, and there are glorious New England fishing villages, museums, historical places, etc., to visit. And there has to be time to rest. And I need to know from Rosita what are the best foods for you to eat, and so many other preparations that we will keep on talking about as we approach the day when we receive you and Rosita at the airport."

An e-mail from Luis to David in late March: *"Mi gran amigo David:*

"The magic tricks came in. Thank you very much. Cesareo and you plant seeds in my mind. I see the marquee already. "Marco the Magi's production of *Le Grand David and his own Spectacular Magic Company* featuring *El Gran Luis,* Cuban Master of the Magic."

"Thanks again my friend!....Bye, I got to go watch the video and practice."

And three days later: *"Buen amigo Cesareo:*

"Preparing to travel to see friends is exhilarating. When it includes baseball it is mind boggling.

"I am so glad David and you have arranged a Red Sox game for us. There could not be a bona fide visit unless we go to a ball game together. Cubans and baseball. *La pelota. "Cuando Minoso batea de verdad, la bola baila un cha-cha-cha..."*

162

Given the way Cesareo functions, it should come as no surprise that Cesareo's new friendship was a company-wide event. Luis was welcomed into the life of El Teacher's theatre company. He received e-mails from the Spanish speaking members of the company, he learned early on that his e-mails to Cesareo were read by everyone (there is a place at the box office for "must reads"), and he received and immersed himself in the three books by and about the company. Every two weeks he received the new issue of the theatre newspaper. Thus, when he arrived in Boston in June, he would know each member of the company by name and personal history. He began to benefit from having a large group of friends in Beverly for months before he ever met them.

Later in March he sent his itinerary for a six-day stay in early June and added: "Reality check: I feel and look good—pictures coming soon—my hair and smile are back 100% and I have resumed a normal life. But my energy level marches to another drummer, and am told it'll take a while to regain full thrust. I can go all day without a nap, but will feel it. Although I know that adrenaline will carry me well in Beverly, baby steps may be good for the first visit after all. Reluctantly."

"Buen Amigo Luis,"

"Yes, baby steps are perfect for me. Remember, I am sixty-eight years old, need a nap everyday, take lots of medication to be able to keep the strength of life going, and slow down many times a day." Cesareo asked Luis to extend his planned visit by two days so that he could see the Larcom show.

Luis responded that Rosita, his son, and daughter-in-law had counseled him to consider carefully the consequences of extending himself too much in this trip. "Basically I was clearly reminded of all my physical shortcomings," he wrote, "and told: 'Stop behaving like a child. Level with Cesareo!'"

Luis proceeded to list for Cesareo the details of his medical condition and the limitations which it imposed on his activity. He also mentioned his "mild asthma."

"We still want to come," he wrote, "but as you can see, baby steps are an unavoidable reality. And it seems self-evident that this first trip I shouldn't be too many days away from my habitual surrounds."

Cesareo's response to Luis was stern and loving. First he reminded Luis that a company of thirty stood behind Cesareo, and it included nurses and professional caretakers—"lovely understanding people who love me and take care of me, and they will know how to love you and take care of you. I wholeheartedly believe that the trip is good for your soul, and like my spirit, yours is indomitable."

Cesareo continued by describing his doctor's impressive record in treating asthma—a disease which troubled Cesareo from time to time. "So, stop apologies. Your family counsel can be sure that I am not an idiot, and that all I need to know is the name of the airline, the flight number and the date and hour of arrival to receive you with our warm, open hearts. The happiness of expecting you and Rosita overwhelms me every time I think about it. And you cannot buy me any dinner while you are here. This is my backyard. The slower you are, the happier we all will be." Out of consideration for Luis, Cesareo even offered to schedule a visit to church to pray with him.

After Luis wrote that he had bought a new camera for the trip, Cesareo responded, "Yes, bring your new camera and a camcorder and a tape recorder and anything you want to record your experience. Your heart and mind will always be the best recorders. It's all wet around here. But the weather teaches us that with a little bit of patience the spring emerges right out of the middle of the winter. A little bit in here, a little bit in there, and soon it will be what we used to call in Cuba *El Mes de las Flores.* Remember, every day of May the school used to go to the chapel to pray to rejoice in the fundamental principal that life rebounds again and again, and again and again."

Luis began to write an article about rediscovering Cesareo:

> You see, once upon a time in a far away land, Cesareo had been a young English teacher at our school. The Marist brothers—a religious order originally from France dedicated to education—were in charge, but some of the teachers were civilians like Cesareo. We knew he was different from all the others; he had passion in his voice, was demanding and seemed to be engaged in an endless pursuit of excellence. Of course, this approach initially made us wish for someone more inclined to a softer pace. Frankly, we would have happily settled for lower expectations— at that age we didn't know any better—but this line of thought didn't fly. And ultimately we were very fortunate; we learned to respect his intensity and integrity, we understood he cared about us. These days I comb gray hairs too, and realize that Cesareo and his extraordinary dedication were the main reason we spoke English fairly well by the time we got here. He made us better, and it helped everyone significantly.

Luis also described his flight from Cuba:

> I took to sea in a small boat with four companions in the middle of the night. Several days later, exhausted after a rough tropical storm had swamped the boat, we managed to land in a remote, barren and uninhabited island in the Gulf Stream. We owe our lives to the dedicated airmen and sailors of the U.S. Coast Guard who spotted us from a seaplane, dropped survival supplies, and later took us to Key West on their vessel. All is well that ends well . . .

Luis arrived in Boston a little after 5 p.m. on June 7, 2001. David was the first to recognize him as the passengers entered the terminal, "There's Luis, Cesareo!" He was walking alone and unassisted. An airline attendant followed him with a wheelchair. Cesareo and Luis embraced.

Luis brought his movie and still cameras and filmed everything "for Rosita," who was unable to accompany him. Conversations around a kitchen table were captured with clicks and whirs, as were his encounters with company members, all of whose names, faces and stories he had learned well before touching down at Logan airport. He could quote chapter and verse from the three volumes published by the company. They talked about the school, what had happened to it and to the brothers. They shared stories about Brother Mauro, about how once the father of a student fell ill and could no longer afford the tuition, so he pulled his son out. Brother Mauro, who could be very strict, went to the father and told him he could not do that. He then arranged for the student to complete his schooling there free. When Catholic clergy were expelled from Cuba in 1961, Brother Mauro had moved to another Latin American teaching assignment.

Luis knew the Maristas retirement community in Guatemala where Brother Mauro was spending his last days, and Cesareo sent him a copy of *Variedades,* one of the books Cesareo had published about his company.

There was something very Cuban about the affection Luis had for the magic company before even arriving here, and the love with which Cesareo embraced him. The culture from which Cesareo and Luis came fostered closeness—a tradition of touching, holding, hugging, and bringing others into one's family. Luis became a member of Cesareo's big Beverly family, and Luis brought the magic company into his family and Cuban tradition that he loved. David received a beautiful certificate making him an honorary Cuban. Just as Cesareo had opened a pipeline of *Le Grand David* materials from Beverly to Miami, Luis opened up one for Cuban tidbits that flowed back to Beverly.

Cesareo had arranged for his good friend Blas Moreno to stay with Luis during his first days in Beverly so that he would feel the security of having a Cuban doctor close at hand. Now a retired Rhode Island physician, Blas discovered Cesareo and company twenty-five years ago and has been a good friend and regular booster ever since. He has a way of communicating a sense of reassurance. In his company you tend to feel healthy. Luis, who had brought his medical records with him (just in case), was able to express his concerns about his health to Blas privately. In the course of the weekend the good doctor looked over his records and put him at ease. "Luis is fine and his recovery has been successful," he told him, Cesareo, and others, and he was right.

Cesareo and David spent many hours talking with Luis, many of them at the kitchen table. There Luis spread out a few treasured rarities—photographs. Cuban exiles left their island so quickly, there usually was no time to gather the little things. For someone like Cesareo, unexpected pictures from youth can contain the power of an atomic bomb, blowing the doors off sealed compartments. Realities that were locked away because of their painfulness now overwhelm like shock waves. In remembering, Cesareo cried.

Hand-painted portrait of
Luis Puello.

Marco's signature
Floating Table.

Clockwise from upper left:
Enrique Machado, Luis
Puello, Valentin Hernandez,
Alberto Bermudez, and
Alberto de Jongh (center).

Elisa at the piano while
visiting Beverly.

Marco asking the audience's
assistance to help him float
the table.

Avrom and Elisa - the rest
is commentary.

From left: Dr. Blas Moreno, Elisa, Cesareo and
Avrom in the lobby of the Cabot.

Chapter Sixteen: A Cuban Album One

The next year, when Cesareo arrived at his hotel in Miami to celebrate Elisa's seventy-fifth birthday, Luis, Valentino (a mortgage broker), and Alberto (who had recently sold his New Orleans based construction company) were there to meet him in one of the lobbies of the plushly carpeted and richly appointed Fountainebleu Hotel. The three Marista alumni stood in front of the softly lit, deeply hued mahogany counters, while Valentino quoted Cesareo's old lectures on economic value line and verse. Alberto recalled how Cesareo had accurately lampooned one of his classmates for his lackadaisical attitudes.

"You taught us English, and that was the most practical thing we learned, although at the time who would have thought so? We called you 'El Teacher.'" Valentino said. Luis recalled how Cesareo had taught the language partly through song. "You taught us 'Oh Susannah.'"

Another Marista had recently e-mailed Cesareo his recollections of a show Cesareo had decided to stage for Mother's Day in the school. He went from classroom to classroom recruiting singers. He wrote,

> "There was already a school choir, but you wanted other people—not from the choir. When you arrived in my classroom, you looked at me and asked, 'Why don't we try your voice?'
>
> "I told you no because that is a waste of time. Your reaction was, NOTHING IS LOST IN TRYING, so

I agreed to the test. To make a long story short, you accepted me as a tenor.

"Under your direction each part rehearsed and rehearsed. One day at last we all got together to hear what 'El Teacher's' choir sounded like. Well, the first time—according to you—was not so bad. But the day before the celebration, that was horrible. I can't tell you how it sounded, because I couldn't hear the other voices while I sang—something, by the way, that I can do now. The point is that you said, 'IF THIS IS A GIFT THAT YOU ARE GOING TO GIVE YOUR MOTHER, THEN-YOU-DO-NOT-HAVE-MOTHERS!' You pulled no punches, and insulted our mothers to boot.

"The next day when we arrived to perform for the Mother's Day celebration, we looked at each other and thought about what our teacher said. The show began and, when we finished, the applause was enough to knock the school down. Right there I lost my fear of the the audience. It was a triumph for all of us. After that, I dove into music and it has become one of the great loves of my life."

When Luis first contacted Cesareo, the Book of Magic illusion was on the drawing boards and about to be built for *An Anthology of Stage Magic* at the Larcom Theatre. Based on an illusion staged by Fu Manchu, Cesareo created a version that is very personal. As one of his front curtain solos entered its final minutes, the haunting *intermedio* from Ernesto Lecuona's zarzuela *Rosa La China* began. The backdrop rose to show clowns leaning in slumber against

170

a six-foot-tall book with a colorful dragon painted on its cover. Cesareo clapped his hands to awaken them, and they carried the book to a portal center stage in a circular dance.

The book was hung on this portal, and as the clowns opened it the *intermedio* broke into its rumba section. The open book revealed portraits of Katie, Webster and Marian on the left page. Cesareo danced up to the book and blew a kiss to Martha's portrait on the right-hand page. Now fourteen years old, she had just gone away to her first year at prep school. Cesareo has given her a place of honor because he promised her that she would continue to be there with him in every show *(siempre en ma corazon)*.

As the rumba continued, the clowns opened the book to pages four and five. There are the portraits of five women of the company, with C U B A spelled out along the bottom. This ornate design features typical Cuban vegetation and wild birds, such as colorful parrots and toucans. Cesareo continued to direct and to move with the rumba as the clowns opened pages six and seven—portraits of clowns and musicians of the company.

As the moving music entered its finale, the book opened to the last pages, showing Cesareo and faithful Blacky. Facing them is a life-sized full-body portrait of Le Grand David, painted in the same black and white tuxedo he wears as he magically appears in person from the Book onto the Larcom stage. The curtain falls to the audience's applause as the Book is closed.

When Cesareo's sister Elisa saw the Larcom and Cabot shows for the first time in 1999, the Book of Magic had not yet been built. Over the years, Cesareo had kept her apprised of the goings-on in Beverly. She rejoiced at his successes from her new home in Miami.

Her first evening in Beverly, Elisa seated herself at the piano in the Larcom rehearsal studio and played *la musica Cubana* for her brother. "I cried, it was so beautiful," Cesareo told his friends. Rick, who was with them that evening, remembers, "She played with such passion and intensity that her music coursed through me. It felt fresh, alive, and overpowering, as if she were discovering the music there and then, right with us."

She saw both the Cabot and Larcom shows and was the first to her feet to lead the standing ovation at their final curtains. She loved what she saw and recognized her brother's hand in practically everything. Each of us could sense that she sized people up in an instant and repaid their affection for her brother with her own. She had been the director of the conservatory in Santa Clara and at heart was a music teacher, offering observations and suggestions to the company musicians.

In honor of Elisa's visit, the company met in the Grand Salon for dinner Sunday evening. She played Lecuona (*Muneca de Cristal,* some of the *Danzas Afro-Cubanas* and *Andalucia),* then *Tico Tico* at lightning speed, a potpourri of rumbas, congos and *guarachas* which were the spectacular dance numbers with which Mirre's Follies climaxed their shows—all with a syncopated fiery left hand and soaring melodic right. In some of them, she suddenly stopped, and paused, and then, without losing the rhythm, returned. This was done dramatically in *Quiereme Mucho,* which Cesareo requested.

Like her brother, her conversation was often incisive; her observations had his no-holds-barred perspicacity and acuity. Elisa required the same honesty and alertness from you, and any sign of slow-footed thinking was skewered instantly. Like Cesareo, she could take charge of any situation by virtue of her intelligence. She confided,

"As all young Cuban women, we were always chaperoned. And I never accepted a date without Cesareo's approval. This was our custom, and it stood me in good stead."

Elisa received a steady diet of news from Beverly. Packages to her often included a recently published poster and always a copy of the latest issue of the theatre's paper. Working on the newspaper had always included an activity that directly connected Cesareo to his childhood home in Santa Clara. For practically every issue going back to 1976 he had worked silently, hour upon hour, with a small pair of scissors, precisely and attentively cutting out figures from photos of the shows in order to make collages for the paper. One is reminded of the boy Mirre cutting out figures from his mother's and aunt's old magazines in order to create his miniature toy theatre company, which traveled as a caravan along the floors of his house. Now it is pictures of company members he is arranging lovingly and patiently in new contexts each time. Consequently, each collage tells a different story, but with a common theme: this is an extraordinary ensemble performing a show so beautiful and surprising that you will want to see it. The collages are filled with humor, sometimes by mixing scale (large figures next to small ones), sometimes by surprisingly placing the clowns into scenes. They highlight the star qualities and stage presence of David, Marco and the others. Through collage, Cesareo takes what is familiar and makes it fresh. Each collage is done lovingly and with great affection for the individual characters. He has made at least one quarter-, half-, or full-page collage for practically every issue of the newspaper, published 26 times each year for thirty years.

"Isn't that beautiful! What do you think?" he asks from time to time and invites Rick and others to enjoy the composition. His devotion to his work and satisfaction with its completion is sincere and springs from deep within.

One morning Cesareo stood back from a design that featured the Escape from Stocks illusion. The photo showed him pilloried, with a chorus of pallid masked figures following the action from upstage. The masks are interesting in the sense that they erase facial features. The masked figures actually appear to be faceless or, better yet, completely anonymous. Downstage another group of witnesses, these with monstrous heads and colorful robes.

"In this illusion my head is on the block, just as when I was forced to leave Cuba. I may not have been aware of this when I choreographed it, but in a sense the 'apparitions' represent the people who were lined up shouting obscenities and mocking us as we walked along the tarmac to the airplane. They wanted my head."

In earlier years, Cesareo used to lift the Stocks off the floor by his neck and dance about the stage, as if to tell the audience that this apparatus, designed to incarcerate and mock, was going to be an instrument of his triumph. And suddenly, voila!, he has escaped. Although the audience doesn't know how, it rejoices at the sudden turn with huge applause.

"The apparitions I transformed into colorful witnesses," Cesareo continued. "Each of their gowns is of a different color, but they all wear the same heads. Even their gloves are the same color as the gown." Long, billowing gowns cover everything, nothing of the body is visible. Their movements are swift and almost menacing, yet restrained. They are there to witness, the magic has called them into being, and they are its testament.

"This is how this show has helped me to transform that nightmare into something that is also dramatic, but now it is inspiring. There was, after all, something magical about my escape from Cuba. It was an intense loss as well."

Carnivale was one of Cesareo's favorite traditions. During the festival it was customary to don masks and sing and dance in the streets. It was exhilarating; from behind the protection of the mask surprising and authentic expressiveness emerged. Once he spoke of the unforgettable year when Elisa decided she was going to ride in their *carnivale* parade as a mermaid. "She was truly a mermaid. She wore a costume replete with golden scallops that looked just like fish scales. It was true artistry. To keep it intact, one of my friends and I had to carry her from our home to the parade and lift her onto the float. What a wonderful memory!"

He spoke about how Ernesto Lecuona's Cuban dance *La Comparsa* perfectly captures the way the procession's band could be heard in the distance, barely perceptible. Then as it marched closer, the music grew louder. Often the *cabezudos* or "big heads" were part of the parade. These were costumed characters with huge papier maché heads—the heads themselves were sometimes five feet tall. The head was often a magnificently accurate caricature of its bearer. Not long after *Le Grand David* debuted, the "big heads" made their appearance in the show. The three of them are on stage to bear witness to the Enchanted Flower Vase.

Once a television interviewer asked Cesareo to speak about some of the magic he saw as a child, especially the magician Richiardi. Cesareo had seen his shows, in particular one set in a Dutch motif that featured wooden clog dancing. Cuba had a similar dance called the *chancletera,* and Cesareo sang its music. His love for the clack, clack, clack of the dance led to the inclusion of a tap dance in his staging of the Broom Suspension in the Cabot show.

Asked how he designs a show, Cesareo responded, "I trust my non-rational processes. Deep within me there is an illusion. My illusion. Of happiness. Of providing something of value to others. My own private, secret illusion that leads me through exile—in Spanish this word is *destierro,* which literally means uprooted—into a new home and new community, an illusion I hold for myself and others—perhaps I may call it a dream. It keeps me alive when I have nothing. A dream to form a magic company, buy a theatre, and create something beautiful.

"For magic is why things are so beautiful. Magic is about secrets. Secret is a word that implies quiet, tranquil, unique, out of the public view, silent and protected within." In his voice-over which introduces the Cabot show, Cesareo tells the audience in a whispered confidence, "And now, we begin in silence" [tapering off the final sibilant gently].

Cesareo has often commented that one of the best ways to care for oneself is to care for others. Over the years he has donated literally thousands of tickets to facilities that serve disadvantaged children and adults. Their group leaders send letters to the theatre that often begin, "to whom it may concern" and go on, "We are a temporary shelter for children in the legal custody of the state who have been removed from the care of a parent or guardian with the purpose of stabilizing the child's situation. . ." Another writes, "The children in our program often come from broken homes and unsafe environments."

176

When they enter the theatre, these children look as if they did not belong to where they came from, nor do they belong to where they are going. They shuffle into the lobby baffled and apprehensive, yet you detect that they are "up for it." Somehow, they are willing to give it a shot, even though they have no expectations. Yet, after the show, they look like the rest of the audience—happy, upbeat, and perhaps a little incredulous that a stage magic show could have the happy effect on them that it just had.

Remembering how a new world opened for him when he saw his first stage magic production on his father's knee as a child, Cesareo performs with the wish that these children experience moments of hope, real hope, the kind that works miracles in people's lives.

For one particular morning matinee for schoolchildren, the audience came from an especially poor and crime-ridden city. From the very beginning they sat in awe. Silence blanketed them like new-fallen snow. As the safety curtain rose, you could hear them gasp. For the first several numbers there were more gasps and tremendous applause. After about a half hour, one could sense that they were transported. It is likely that for many of them this was their first live stage show.

The children had come in dozens of school buses and the exit from the theatre at the end is very well organized by the ushering staff. For those who board their buses last, the wait at their seats can last for ten minutes or more. Ping Pong and Li'l Av stand at either side of the stage to protect it from the curious and to help with decorum. Cesareo usually comes through the auditorium after he changes and freshens up after the show. This morning a class of Spanish speaking children were still at their seats waiting to board their bus (which had not yet arrived). They were making a big fuss over Ping Pong and Li'l Av and the clowns were having fun with them. As Cesareo approached, he informed them in Spanish that this was his native language and that he was very happy to see them. Immediately a young boy asked him, "From where?"

"Soy Cubano," Cesareo responded.

Ping Pong and Li'l Av knew instantaneously that this was going to be unforgettable, both because of the light-speed swiftness with which these children were responding to Cesareo, and because in all the years the clowns have known him, they had never once heard him answer a casual interlocutor that he was from Cuba.

And after Cesareo's response, the children began to gather around him and tell him where they were from, like so many kernels of popcorn exploding one after the other. This one is from Mexico, that one from Jamaica, Puerto Rico and Nicaragua. The clowns were very touched by the sincerity of what was happening and by how Cesareo was providing these children with something of value that might go with them for the rest of their lives. Visibly moved, Ping Pong had taken a couple of steps back. One of the children went to him and said in English, "Look, you have a magic white glove. It can make things disappear too," as he gestured towards a tear falling from Ping Pong's painted eye.

Marco, Ping Pong, with the apparitions
in foreground and background.

Marco in Escape from Stocks with David and Ellen.

A comic moment before entering the stocks.

Marco at the Larcom.

Chapter Seventeen: Response to National Tragedy

Each summer the company takes a vacation from performing in August. It was during August in 2001 that David injured his knee in a backstage accident. Since recovery would take several months, Cesareo began to have some of the younger members of the company learn his part in the more strenuous illusions, although he would continue to perform where his special skills were required.

Cesareo had been looking forward to an early September vacation in Florida. After his return he would continue with plans for the twenty-fifth anniversary celebration in five months' time. He had arranged to meet Luis Puello, Rosita, and Enrique for luncheon in Naples, Florida.

The beach was deserted. Cesareo had arrived during an outbreak of red tide. The airborne toxins made breathing difficult and he could have returned to Beverly right away, but he wanted to meet his Cuban friends. They had agreed to meet on Tuesday, September 11, 2001.

"As I set out for the visit that morning, I stopped by a flower shop to buy a red rose corsage for Rosita. As I was getting the flowers, the young woman in the shop, hands trembling, crying, told me the news," Cesareo recalled.

The scheduled opening of the company's twenty-fifth season was postponed for a week. Not only were all the airports closed after September 11, but a near-hurricane struck the southwest coast of

Florida. The winds knocked out electricity. After cancellations of four different flight itineraries, Cesareo managed to get to Manchester, New Hampshire, via Philadelphia and arrived in Beverly at 1:30 a.m. Sunday, September 16.

The company was at the Cabot early that morning. As the sun illuminated the marquee, the name *Le Grand David* was not on it. The marquee simply said: God Bless America.

Dr. Ruff commented that during this time he monitored Cesareo's metabolism closely, because the September 11 attacks were bound to trigger traumatic memories. Work always seems to be Cesareo's antidote. He had designed a new opening for the show in the silent hours spent flying to Beverly. He wrote to Henry Lewis that he was moved by "the tension of sadness and hope reminding me the show must go on." He asked Henry whether he had ever seen a magic show that began with seven sustained minutes of silence. "This is what the show will be for us in our twenty-fifth year. We will remember."

Typically Cesareo directs from the inside out. He prepares conditions for the actor to go within himself or herself, rather than being told what to do from the outside by someone else. The action then springs from within. This Sunday morning, Cesareo began by having the cast move through the opening choreography without music. They were asked to pair off, to mirror their partners on the other side of the stage, to sense what everyone else was doing. From this sensitivity the ensemble was to establish its own tempo.

When someone protested that a curtain pull had been based on a particular musical cue, Cesareo responded, "Find another cue. There is no music. We are now doing it without music."

One company member recalled, "Suddenly it was a new world." Yet because of the way Cesareo had begun the rehearsal, this realization came from within. The actors had already created this choreography in silence from within themselves.

At the season premier a week later, the new opening began while the house lights were still up with a recorded announcement required by the laws of Massachusetts. Cesareo's voice directed the audience to notice the location of the exits, to proceed to them in case of an emergency and walk away from the building. Cesareo then ended the statement with the words, "And now the show will begin in silence . . ."

Masked figures descended the left and right aisles from the back of the auditorium. As the house lights dimmed, the figures slowly ascended the elegant steps to the edges of the proscenium. They remained there motionless, subtly illuminated by pin spots. By now the house lights were off, and the spots on these figures gently bled onto the edges of the front curtain. In silence, the figures still did not move. The front safety curtain rose. Then a gold lamé curtain scalloped upward to present a frieze of masked mythological figures and unmasked goddesses, who moved slowly in front of a curtain embroidered with oriental scenes. After all exited, two goddesses remained circling about each other, holding ancient banners. The Oriental curtain parted to reveal a deep brown, red and gold curtain embroidered with a large dragon, which opened while the Oriental was still parting. All this was done in silence.

Visible now, a golden stair descended from an Oriental tea house set against the back wall of the stage. A half dozen maidens holding fans entered from sliding doors on the stage level of the tea house, protected by handsome marshals bearing pennons. The silence was broken briefly by a distant trumpet intoning a line from "America, the Beautiful." Down the stairs came more masked figures, maidens and princes. Finally, enshrouded in cloaks, Le Grand David and Marco the Magi descended the stairs. They tossed off their capes, as the castanets of a rousing orchestral *España Cani* (popular bull fight music) electrified the stage.

The audience at that September 23 performance watched the new opening segue into the customary illusions. The opening scene dissolved into exits while others entered for Doves From the Air, in which Marco and David snatch these lithesome winged beauties out of thin air and place them into cages held by others while a chorus looks on. As this scene atomized, the colorful "rain" curtain had closed towards the rear of the stage to form a background for the next illusion—Magi Without a Middle.

Cesareo as Marco moved downstage right and tore off his kimono as usual and tossed it to Ula la Damisella (Katie). Immediately he tossed her a second, then a third, fourth, fifth—he continued launching kimonos he had been wearing under each other until Ula stood holding a small mountain of them in her arms, and Marco stood there in an old-fashioned red tank-top bathing suit that looked rather like a turn-of-the-last-century pair of red underwear, brandishing the last kimono across his derriere like a shower towel.

As the audience relished the comedy of the Magi in his underwear, Marco galumphed over to David, holding open the door of the mysterious cabinet awaiting him. In he went, facing the audience and waving. David closed the door so that only Marco's head and feet were visible, and slid two wide steel blades through the cabinet at shoulder and waist level, opened the front door, and behold, Marco stood there with no middle. David withdrew the blades, reopened the doors, and voila! Marco, whole, stepped out and melted to the floor to accept an awaiting cape to the rousing conclusion of *España Cani* and a burst of applause. Doves from the Air and Without a Middle together lasted five minutes.

This juxtaposition of reverential silence with rousing music, conjuring and comedy was precisely the effect Cesareo wanted. He explained it in an e-mail to Henry, in which he wrote: "The show now begins with SILENCE. Seven minutes of silence, preceded by the sound of a bronze bell, calling for the silence. Everything is visual, slow and quiet, and suddenly the clapping in the music of *España Cani* returns the show to its now traditional structure, as if saying, 'the light still shines in the darkness, and the darkness has not been able to extinguish it.'"

In another e-mail to Henry, Cesareo wrote more about how he deeply he was experiencing this national tragedy and expressed from another angle the meaning of the seven minutes of silence:

> And the audience came: children, grandparents, lots of couples and adults. President Bush had asked the country to continue normal activities, as much as possible, and people did come to the theatre today. It was a very large audience, unusually respectful from the moment they entered.
>
> It seemed as if a new tone of deeper seeking and reflection had brought down the curtain on any frivolity of preceding times. Some forms of entertainment seem beside the point now. A sober tone was there. Suddenly, in the middle of the silent

movements, I had arranged for a trumpet, far away, to play a phrase from "America, The Beautiful." ("America, America, God shed His grace on thee.") And after, silence again.

This second silence was deep and penetrating. A respectful mood filled the air. I could sense the theatre like a cathedral. For me, all the souls of magic were here today.

Then, *España Cani:* the sound of the castanets, the clapping and *taconeo* that precedes the trumpets announcing the opening of the bullfight that leads to the *paso doble* that initiates the Birds from the Air, all that could barely be heard. The audience was applauding as if they were telling us, "Yes, yes, yes, we are with you."

When the first bird appeared from the air, I could barely see it through my the tears. As I began to take my kimonos off to enter the Magi Without a Middle illusion, I wondered, how could I continue being funny in this everything-has-changed-atmosphere? This time the sounds I have heard in twenty-five years of disrobing were different. I sensed a quiet decorum. At the end of Without a Middle, when I fell to the floor, I realized that they had been applauding before that, ahead of me.

Yes, today, fantasy emerged as a most important category. Obviously, the audience was moved in response to our working on details. We took off all the stroboscopic lights and similar effects, and went for gentle, soothing lights and colors. They understood.

Henry Lewis responded, "I am reminded of the words of Sir Walter Scott, who wrote, 'Under all speech that is good for anything there lies a silence which is better. Silence is deep as Eternity; speech is as shallow as time.'"

John Fisher received a message from Cesareo that included the following: "See, John, we are attempting to redefine the language of magic. What is entertainment? What is fun? What are the proper jokes that invite laughter? What is the meaning of magic when we stand next to six thousand dead bodies?

"We trust that people will be equally capable of finding similar intensities of meaning while we perform our magic. I, thereby, want to denote the intrinsic fact that being human always relates and points to something other than itself. To bear witness to the human potential at its best, is to turn tragedy into triumph. As Plutarch once put it: 'The measure of a man is the way he bears up under misfortune.'"

David Goodsell wrote to Cesareo, "I am sure that you have a better sense of the value of liberty than the rest of us do, even after this tragedy. I have always felt that *Le Grand David and his Own Spectacular Magic Company* was not just a return to the great Latin American magic shows of the past, as marvelous as it has always been. It has seemed to me that it was also a personal statement from you about the human spirit. It is an inspiration to me. I have shed many a tear this past week."

185

Cesareo received the following e-mail from Michael Bailey, the President of The Magic Circle in London:

September 18, 2001

Dear Cesareo,

We all felt an indescribable sadness as we watched with heightening horror the terrible events of 11th September. Whether we were near or far from this catastrophe of evil, we shared the shock and the effects have—or will—reach us all in one way or another.

Your own trials, compounded by the dangerous weather in Florida, demonstrate that the shockwave reached you quickly and made your life difficult. But your re-planning of the opening of the 25th season was a masterly and moving solution. Rightly, you did not cancel but used the moment to gently move the audience gradually from reflection and respect into a new world that would at least take their minds for a while away from the events of just five days previous. You achieved that in a remarkable fashion, whilst allowing everyone to remember in their own way those who had suffered.

Here we are urging a return to normality but we are fearful in our hearts. We have suffered from terrorism here for many years and some of us remember the blitz of the Second World War. My father was manager of a bank in Wimbledon, south west London and we

186

lived 'over the shop'. I was a child then, sleeping every night on the ledger shelves in the bank's strongroom in the basement with its thick walls and strong door. The bombs rained down most nights and we survived.

Churchill was our inspiration and his words of encouragement kept the country going when we were nearly down and out. I was interested to see that President George W. Bush's speechwriters have studied those wartime speeches and even used one or two of the phrases recently.

The world has changed overnight. We shall never forget the fateful 11th September. But we will survive again and win again and maybe become even stronger.

We are thinking of you. Have a successful 25th year.

Michael

The company responded:

October 1, 2001

Dear Michael,

Cesareo was kind enough to share your email with us here in the *Le Grand David Magic Company*. It touches us and reveals to us a very big heart that resonates with our own struggle and sadness and very deeply felt wish to step into this new world securely and triumphantly. Never in our lives could we have imagined such a thing, nor could we have imagined that the supportive expressions of friends could be so uplifting at this time.

The opening of our show has allowed us to become more reflective and more receptive of these realities, and performing it is full of meaning for us. The fact that the show continues in a joyous vein, as it has for so many years now, renews us and, perhaps, our audiences as well. If we can all experience the goodness of life together for two hours, then we have, in a sense, brought something very important to each other. Your words now are woven into the larger fabric of our efforts here. They nurture and fortify, and have become part of us.

In an e-mail to Phil Willmarth, Cesareo wrote "At the Larcom show, we wait for the end. After we've completed the show, staff and cast meet on stage to sing together with the audience the first verse of 'America the Beautiful,' followed by a beautiful fanfare. The audience leaves very touched, and we get a deep sense of gratitude and love for the country."

Chapter Eighteen: A Cuban Album Two

On March 3, 2004, Cesareo received word that Elisa had suffered a heart attack and subsequent stroke. He flew to Miami to be with her. She passed away two days later.

Cesareo wrote to Henry, "I brought back all of sister's sheet music (that she used to play while I sang through the years) for Avrom and the company. Avrom picked out one at random and sight read it for us at the piano. Silently, the lyrics of the song crossed my mind. "Awaken my dear, awaken. The sun is finally shining. The little birds are singing, and the darkness dissolved . . . "

David and Rick made copious notes of a Saturday in March a year later. They set out with Cesareo from southwest Florida for a morning flight to the Marista Reunion Luncheon at La Carreta Restaurant on Calle Ocho, deep in the heart of Miami's "Little Havana." Planning for the trip had begun in earnest three months prior, when it was decided there would be no show on Sunday, March 13, to allow Cesareo ten days of well deserved rest, relaxation and sun. Several inches of snow blanketed Boston's North Shore that day.

For the past several years Luis has worked with persistent diligence and devotion towards the creation of an online network of Maristas from Santa Clara. His MaristaNet newsletters have been carried electronically to alumni around the globe. In the weeks leading up to the reunion, the Internet drums had been thumping out the message that *"El Teacher/El Gran Mago"* was coming to Miami, and word was coming back that the troops were mobilizing.

On the drive to the airport, Cesareo suggested that the day might bring many surprises and said, "For me it's as if we're traveling back in time."

As soon as the landing gear hit the tarmac in Miami, David phoned Luis who, as if waiting for orders, was stationed at a restaurant five minutes from the airport. He pulled up curbside in front of the bustling terminal and, after warm greetings, steered them towards his home in Coral Gables. As they passed through the quiet, palm-shaded residential streets, Luis slowed down, pointed to his right and said to Cesareo, "That is Violeta's house there."

Violeta had taken on near-legendary stature in the stories Cesareo had told about his first theatrical company. The pretty *rumbera* of Mirre's Follies had recently heard of his whereabouts through the Miami grapevine and immediately called him.

"Stop! Stop the car! I want to say hello," was Cesareo's immediate response.

As he approached her door that Saturday morning, Luis related to David and Rick how Violeta had turned her remarkable compassion to adopting and caring for a quadriplegic boy for the past ten years, after raising her own sons.

When Cesareo introduced himself to the housekeeper at the front door, the young woman recognized his name immediately and called out, "Violeta, Cesareo's here!" Violeta's voice could be heard from the back of the house, protesting that she was still in her pajamas and needed time to prepare herself. Cesareo assured the housekeeper that he would return shortly. Luis drove them two blocks further to his house in order that they might call on Luis's wife, Rosita.

Here they were met with similar protestations: from behind closed doors a voice both surprised and alarmed let them know that their audience must await the necessary applications of couture, cosmetics and composure. With a droll delivery worthy of Jack Benny, Luis informed them that they were witnessing typical behaviors of the sophisticated Cuban female.

In the meantime they met Max, a wheezing, prancing, twelve-year-old graybeard of a Chihuahua, who immediately sniffed out David as a simpatico "dog-lover" and hopped into his lap.

In what Luis described as record time, Rosita appeared from her sequestration. Looking every bit *La Damisela Encantadora* (the title of a portrait Cesareo and Rick had painted and sent to her the previous year) and with great warmth and genuine affection, she invited them into her living room. She had not seen Cesareo for four years, and her hospitality and deference to his comfort were awe-inspiring. Refreshments and cookies soon cascaded from the kitchen.

Before too long, a knock came at the front door. Much to their surprise, it was Violeta, who had driven over from her home. After more hugs, kisses and caresses, Violeta alighted on one end of the couch, eyes twinkling and brimming with smiles.

She recounted her years with Cesareo's company in Cuba. Of course David had come prepared with a video camera to record the recollections that friends and former students might have of their days with Cesareo back in Santa Clara. Violeta asked if she could speak in Spanish, because she felt more comfortable that way. Her radiant beauty and vitality bubbled over as she spoke, alternately talking to the camera and to Cesareo.

"Remember, Cesareo, how helpful your Aunt Aurora was making all those ruffled costumes for us: the long train behind my gown with a thousand yellow ruffles on it, each one trimmed in black. And your beautiful shirt with the small ruffles on the sleeves," Violeta said with her gaze far off as if visualizing scenes from long ago.

"Yes," answered Cesareo, "we made several like that for our shows in Beverly. I wear one now during my solo at the Larcom Theatre."

Turning towards Rick, Violeta continued, "And Cesareo's sister, Elisa, would accompany us on the piano. She was amazing. It was like having a professional orchestra backing us." Eyes moistening, she said, "Cesareo, those were the golden days of my life."

After more photos, warm exchanges and arrangements for Violeta to visit Beverly, Cesareo, Luis, David and Rick proceeded to the restaurant, situated on the main thoroughfare of Miami's Cuban district. They parked in front of a modest white-stucco eatery that a tourist might pass by without notice. It seemed to be frequented mostly by the local populace. The pictures on the walls were of nineteenth-century Cuba: a paradise of glorious Spanish architecture, postcard-perfect beaches, and sun-drenched tobacco fields.

They could hear the din from the gathering in the rear function room before they could see it. Clearly, this was not a crowd accustomed to quiet meditations. First in view was the "gentle giant," Luis's dear friend Enrique Machado, who filled the door frame with his towering presence. Enrique and Luis had met Cesareo and his entourage two years previously when they arrived in Miami for Elisa's seventy-fifth birthday party. Luis and Enrique had rented a van to chauffeur them around town and doted over them like mother hens. After Enrique's ninety-year-old mother, for whom he had cared for many years, had passed on, he had flown to Beverly for a stay.

Lingering handshakes, hugs, laughter, backslapping, and shouts of welcome from across the room greeted Cesareo as he was ushered into the commotion. The word spread like wildfire that their former teacher had arrived.

Over forty men were there. Some had brought their wives. Almost all of them had been schoolboys in the mid-fifties, sitting at attention in crisp blue uniforms. An owner of another Cuban restaurant in Miami, Alberto, began singing with others and later vividly recalled learning the lyrics to "Take Me Out to the Ballgame" and "I've Been Working on the Railroad" in Cesareo's class. "This is how he taught us, not only English, but about America," reminisced Alberto. "He got us all singing."

They had gathered together on this special occasion to revel in each other's company. A few had traveled great distances: from Puerto Rico, Colombia, Brazil and Argentina. In small circles they exchanged anecdotes, memories, jokes, and news of recent events on the island of their youth. Though most were by now retired, they had made careers in America as doctors, engineers, businessmen and entrepreneurs. Each had been forced to adapt to a new homeland, come face to face with an uncertain future; most had successfully constructed new lives. "America," one said with tears in his eyes, "is the land of second chances." None are young any more; their hair is gray, and some lean on canes. Many of the wives sweetly commented how their husbands had followed with pride Cesareo's career and accomplishments as a magician.

"Mirre!" cried out one man.

"Pepito!" answered Cesareo. And tears were wiped away with one hand while the other was clasped in an endless handshake. Pepito was in Miami for just fifteen days on a special visa from Santa Clara, Cuba. "It took a lot of paperwork," he said.

Several of the men related stories of dramatic escapes in the wake of Castro's accession. A few in the room had arrived on U.S. shores in the early 1960s under the auspices of Project Pedro Pan, a church-sponsored program that flew youngsters to America with the understanding that their parents would follow as soon as the political climate cooled off. Most never again saw their folks, many of whom died on the island. As one man remarked, "All of them are here because of one thing: freedom." And as Cesareo reflected later, almost in a whisper, "These are the ones who stayed alive." Each was bursting at the seams with half-a-century's worth of stories to tell, compressed into three hours.

At noon, the meal began with a prayer, led by Raphael de los Reyes, the former Olympic basketball star now known simply as "The Deacon." Cesareo, Luis, David, Enrique, and Brother Rafael shared a table. Now an elegant and serene gentleman several years older than Cesareo, Hermano Rafael Martin was a former colleague at the Marista High School who helped Cesareo take asylum in the Colombian embassy and secure a teaching position in Bogotá. When the heaping portions of *arroz con pollo,* fried plantains and sangria were brought forth, Brother Rafael leaned towards Cesareo, "Listen. They are eating. Now there is silence."

But not for long. After an industrial-strength custard was consumed, the roiling commotion again filled the room. Seated at the table to

Cesareo's right was Carlos Villanueva, another Cuban basketball legend. He insisted that they pull their table sideways to link up with his table of eight, effectively blocking the waiters' path. Luis looked at Rick and said, "No problem. It's a Cuban thing!" The table soon became the staging area for a raffle. Holders of the winning tickets carried away copies of *Journey to Freedom,* an account of the Deacon's defection while on tour in Ireland with the Cuban national basketball team.

With just a little prompting, Jorge Ramirez Pedraza, a strapping, former student (and Victor Mature look-a-like) broke into soaring operatic renditions of "O Sole Mio" and "Return to Sorrento." Jorge later told David that the years he spent as a Marista "were the best of times. They just didn't last long enough. I was only sixteen when we left with Project Pedro Pan. It was the last time I saw my parents."

Another former student recounted a scene that Cesareo himself had forgotten. During one of the school's pageants, *"El Teacher"* had played the role of Fr. Champagnat, the founder of the Marista teaching order, later canonized as a saint, and the student played the role of an early student from the 1800s. "I was so nervous," he remembered, "that I was petrified. Barely a muscle moved other than my knees knocking together. You were calm and kept the show going when we forgot our lines or made mistakes. And look at you now! You've gone on to great success on stage."

By 3:00 people began taking their leave. Enrique joined Cesareo and friends in the car. He and Luis proudly gave them the Cook's Tour of posh Coral Gables: the gorgeous homes, the Venetian Pool, the Biltmore Hotel, and historic churches. Luis said to Cesareo, "You made a lot of people happy today." By 4:00 Cesareo was back at the Miami airport.

Through the window of the plane, the cosmopolitan glow of Miami rapidly receded and the dark gray gloom of the everglades shrouded the landscape. Along the horizon, thin bars of deep orange and red delineated Earth from sky, an hour removed from sunset. Before arriving in Miami, they had wondered what awaited them. On the return flight to Tampa and on the drive back to Sarasota, they reflected with thanks and appreciation on what had transpired. As Violeta said earlier in the day, *"Esto es algo para recordar."* (This is quite something to remember.)

Cesareo, in his silence, provided little commentary; these old men were once his students and one could sense their sincere gratitude to him and how much he had meant to them. For eight magical hours, a veil was lifted, and David and Rick got a glimpse of life from another time and another place—now vanished.

Cesareo encapsulated his sentiments in these lines:

> *Remembrance and the sea*
> *will give answer*
> *to the shuttered heart.*
>
> — *The Magician's Obligation*

One Sunday morning four months later, Cesareo called the company together to tell them about Maria Ibanez, a national officer of the Society of American Magicians, who would be seeing the show that afternoon. She had left Cuba with her parents in 1962 at the age of eight and told the story of her exile through a Magic Coloring Book. Cesareo asked a company member to demonstrate how the Magic Coloring Book is usually performed.

First the magician flips through the pages of a paperback book whose cover indicates it is a coloring book. But all the pages are blank. Then he asks the audience to think of magical things, wonderful magical things, and to project them onto the pages of the book. Then he flips through the pages one by one. They now magically contain black and white line drawings of the very things the audience thought of. He flips through the book once more. This time the line drawings are beautifully colored.

After the demonstration, Cesareo continued his narrative about Maria. Through her Coloring Book she describes what it was like to leave Cuba. "Her story allows you to understand me better, because she presents this illusion from the depth of her soul," he said, struggling through tears to project his words. Collecting himself, he continued, "Unlike the usual presentation of this illusion, which is from the outside in (the magician has the audience choose the pictures to appear in the book), she does it from the inside out. She begins by flipping through a book of blank pages. 'This is what it was like to begin again,' she says. 'You bring nothing of life from Cuba. Not your language, not your friends, nor your grandparents, your cousins, your house, your neighborhood, your books, your music, your teachers, school, church, favorite stores, nothing. Gone. So many blank pages.'"

That evening she performed the illusion on the Larcom stage for some members of the company and dignitaries from the Society of American Magicians, who were meeting in Boston that weekend. She told her audience that she entered fourth grade in the United States in May 1962, two or three weeks before the end of the school year. She met Jay Ibanez in that class. They became friends—best friends, and eventually over the years they fell in love and married.

After giving birth to two sons, there was an intense sadness. How could she tell them what it meant to her to be Cuban—so many blank pages. So she went to members of her family in this country and asked for their stories, and recorded them, and now she flips through the coloring book again, and there are black and white drawings and photographs of her parents, grandparents, and great aunts and uncles, and pictures of their life in Cuba.

She began to tell the stories to her sons and in the telling, something miraculous happened. Now she flips through the pages again, and all the pictures are in beautiful color. She opens the book to its last full color page, and there is a photograph of her two adult sons in full military uniform. She is proud.

From the silence of treasured memory vaults, Rene (Cesareo's boyhood friend and the *rumbero* of Mirre's Follies) made contact with him in February 2005. Cesareo at once sent him the three hardbound volumes about the magic company and a selection of posters. Rene began planning a visit to Beverly with his wife, Clotilde. The magic company completed its twenty-ninth season anticipating his visit. Rene and Clotilde finalized plans to see the show a week before Cesareo's seventy-third birthday in October. When Rene's cousin Dominguito got wind of this, he signed on and flew from his home in Chicago for the reunion.

Friday evening, Ann welcomed Rene and Clotilde while Cesareo, David and Avrom met Dominguito at the airport. When the car pulled into the driveway a couple of hours later Rene and Clotilde ran from the house to embrace Cesareo, and then everyone was embracing everyone else. They broke into songs they used to sing onstage, Clotilde joined them, and soon Rene and Dominguito's cameras were going to work. The syncopations of congos and cha cha chas were accented by flash bulbs. Rene is average height and build, with almond eyes that squeeze into a squint when he smiles and a lively head of white hair. Clotilde is slender, pretty, with fiery black eyes, black eyelashes, and the power of a hurricane at her fingertips. She is quick to smile and gracious. Dominguito is tall and thin, bald, with dark eyes that penetrate and yet abruptly break into a dance of happiness. His lips easily curl into a broad smile, and his hearty laugh rises from the depths of his throat.

The party moved into the house and settled around the piano, where Clotilde lavished the group with Cuban melodies, beginning with *La Habanera Tu.* She is an extraordinary pianist, trained in the conservatory; she played beautifully even though she commented that she hadn't played for thirty-five years. Cesareo's conversation with them naturally fell into Spanish, the language of their youthful jokes, confidences and now recollections. Once in a while Rene or Clotilde's voice would emerge from the happy cacophony to translate a particular phrase or the last sentence for the non-Spanish speakers. Then Cesareo might begin speaking Spanish to one of the company members, who would have to ask, Cesareo, English please. What joy and happiness! Rene, Clotilde and Cesareo are natural entertainers and they share with Dominguito an enormous love for their musical and theatrical traditions.

After dinner Cesareo asked Rick to meet the group at the Larcom. Rene had not only read, but had studied the three published volumes, and from time to time during the tour of the galleries and the theatre, connected what he had read to what he was seeing. His initial impression and comment at the end of the evening was, "I am shocked. Even though I have read about all of this, to see it is an entirely different matter. This beauty, order, elegance and perfection are beyond anything I could have imagined."

Rene talked about his brother Pedro, who had greatly helped Rene and his family come to the United States and settle here. Cesareo learned of how Pedro had courageously faced his death in the mid 80s and he cried.

On Sunday Rene, Clotilde and Domingo arrived at the theatre and were seated in the row five, from which Cesareo originally directed the show. They may have helped to inspire others, because the audience response to the show was overwhelming.

After the show the three of them lingered in the auditorium and greeted every cast member as he or she returned from the lobby bidding adieu to the audience. They joined the company on stage for photos, and then Clotilde sat down at the piano at the front of the auditorium and began to play improvised piano versions of some of the songs the barbershoppers had sung during the show. She had confessed Friday evening that she had such a love for playing popular music by ear that she drove her classical teachers crazy as a child. After she played, the barbershoppers gathered around the piano and serenaded her. She danced as they sang. The company gathered about the three of them and exchanged stories.

The next morning Rene had this to say:

> The curtain rises, immediately you hear the music and it flows about you like the air you breathe. Then the show kicks up. It's like a relaxing therapy. Everyone is so involved and thrown into the plot of the show that there is a connection among each of

them and everything happens so softly and smoothly that you feel totally relaxed. It is the most beautiful feeling that you can have. And then the music—the selections have been so properly chosen that they blend with everything. I mean, it is mind boggling, to tell you the truth, what you have accomplished here. You know you have good stuff, but you are part of it. We are from the outside looking in and it's really wonderful to behold.

Cesareo is beyond description, because you know the talent is there. It has matured, yet the demeanor on stage remains exactly the same. He commands the stage in the way he relates to the actors and actresses. The interaction with the public—as soon as he opens his mouth and throws a few a words out he wraps up the audience and they become part of the show. This is all as it was in our youth. So he hasn't changed, he has just matured in his golden age. I am in awe of what I saw yesterday.

The hospitality of every single member of the company, how they greet you with warmth and sincerity—you can feel it in the handshake, in the embraces, you feel that you are really welcome. It's a welcome that sinks into your soul and into your heart.

The fluidity and the grace that David has onstage is amazing. It's like sometimes he's gliding, he's floating—it's the elegance of his gestures, it is something I have never seen in anyone performing magic. It's not a false routine that he has created, it is smooth, spontaneous, fluid, elegant, expressive.

One thing that is beautiful, also, is how the ladies tell the stories before two of the illusions, like preparing the audience for what is about to come. And there is little bit of everything that is beautiful in theatre, including a little bit of vaudeville, dance, mime, a complex of things intertwined and so smoothly done. It's not just the magic, but it is the background, the costumes, and how softly the entrances project into the audience. Children and adults alike were taken by it. All I wish for all of you is to continue with health and with the enthusiasm and energy that you have put into it—to continue having this success. These things do not happen often.

Dominguito added:

This is a work of love, no false handshake, false smile, these are people I am happy to relate to. One thing that impressed me most was the humility of Cesareo. He tried to have the second place, he didn't try to dominate what was going on, he treats everyone very fairly on stage. His relationship with David, like a father, looking at what is going on, as if to say, I want to be sure that everything is right, but I am not going to take credit. So the show belongs to everyone in the cast. Here everyone is capable to take the lead at times. This is very unique. It is everybody's work, that is amazing. No one is trying to steal the show. It is just the opposite.

The show goes without words, that was very impressive. Everyone seems to be speaking, everybody seems to be very communicative, but they are communicating without words. This is a song without words.

And Clotilde:

The show is perfect when you do not realize that time goes by. You're there, you experience each member of the cast during the show, you have an immediate rapport with each actor. In children it is very difficult because their span of concentration is very limited, and yet, they were in ecstasy, they were magically involved in that world that was created and did not move from their seats.

One other thing I am compelled to say—the way we left our country and how everything was taken away from us. No one can take what you learn, and no one can take from you what you lived through your life. That is the only thing that you can take with you. No matter where you are in life. And Cesareo has proved it here in Beverly. The way that he learned, the music that he heard, the magic that he saw, the imagery and beauty of our native land, what he learned with his friends and in his family, no one can take from him. He was able to serve others through what came from his unforgettable life in his own country, and that's our life in exile.

When it came time for leavetaking, it was emotional and brief. Cuban Americans tend to make their goodbyes as lighthearted and swift as they can, because they have all experienced the agony of a departure that lasts a lifetime, at least one lifetime.

Rene Perez Bode and Mirre - a unique theatricality.

Violeta y Mirre 55 years later.

Painted backdrop of Marco (left) and
David at the Larcom Theatre.

A lasting friendship: Cesareo and Ray Goulet
in the lobby of the Cabot.

Chapter Nineteen: Victory of the Spirit

As the company prepared to perform its February 27, 2005, show, Ann, who is Cesareo's dresser, was wondering how he was feeling. Being his dresser means helping to prepare his costumes for each number, assisting with the changes, having water and juice available for him, and medications, if needed.

The two-hour-and-fifteen-minute Cabot show is more physically demanding on him than the Larcom show, according to Ann. The Thursday night prior he had performed the Larcom show, and even though he wasn't feeling all that well, the audience never knew.

So, Friday night while ushering for the film, Ann's antennae were out gauging Cesareo's health. What she was seeing was not encouraging. Everyone in the company is aware of his chronic heart condition and the medications he takes for it. A cold or even worse—flu-like symptoms—can take a big toll on him. By Saturday his condition was not improved, and she was relieved that he stayed at home to rest and did not come to the theatre that evening, as he usually does.

Sunday morning his congestion had not abated. He was economical in his movements and speech, his voice was thin and breathing seemed shallow. Nevertheless he rehearsed Ellen and Li'l Av in a new twist for the Escape from the Stocks illusion that would make it seem even more surprising and more flamboyant, something that would set the audience's gums a-tingling.

Just prior to the show David advised members of the cast to be prepared to catch Cesareo if he faltered while descending the twenty-foot staircase from the Oriental tea-house to open the show, saying, "Today his sense of balance is a little dodgy, as our British friends would say."

As the large audience filled the house a little before 3:00, Ann kept her car key handy and she was parked close to the stage door so that she could drive Cesareo to the hospital if need be. He was going to do the show, and intended to do the whole thing; however, it was prudent to be prepared for an adverse turn.

The opening curtain rose; Cesareo began his descent. One step, two, three, four, and there was a hesitation. As he collapsed, a dozen hands caught him and kept him from hitting the floor. David's voice rang out, "Push him forward!" Suddenly he was up. He told the concerned company to let him go and completed the descent by himself. All this in five seconds, maybe less. He continued with his usual choreography in Birds from the Air, as did the rest of the company, and then he moved into the next illusion, the Magi Without a Middle. At its completion he stepped out of the illusion "whole and restored" to a thunderous applause, and exited with his usual stage-spanning artistry.

He enters again two illusions later for a brief two-minute solo to teach the audience their trick while a set change occurs behind the curtain. But today, before teaching them the trick, he spoke privately with the audience. He told them that he had fallen during the opening (which they had seen), and that the company caught him. "See how much they love me? In case you are wondering how old I am, I'm seventy-two years old. And now, would you like to learn a trick?"

After he finished to a large applause, the curtain opened for the next number—Happy and Healthy. Cesareo cavorted about the stage with a juggler and the Owl, played by Igor, who said later, "I was moved by Cesareo's efforts. I could tell he was struggling with all his might to hold himself together."

The show continued as usual, except one thing was different. Company members knew that Cesareo had practically no physical strength. We saw that each movement was requiring gargantuan effort from him. It was absolutely clear that what was keeping him going was his determination to hold his own, his love for the show and for the company that was performing it with him, and his lifelong habit of going beyond himself and usual limits. Cesareo has called it "the victorious way of the spirit."

It's an hour and forty-five minutes until intermission, and Cesareo performed every single step. The Escape from the Stocks is towards the end of the first half. It is Cesareo who enters the stocks and later magically frees himself. The new twist rehearsed the day before required a rapid movement by Cesareo to fling the cloth—which is six feet by eight feet and weighs five pounds easily—over his head and behind him. As Cesareo's hands and neck were locked into the Stocks, Ellen and Li'l Av lifted the cloth as rehearsed—up, sway, back. As they placed the cloth over the imprisoned Magi—whoof! It was as if a genie had suddenly appeared. Cesareo yanked the cloth out of their hands and flung it to the back of the stage to reveal himself standing free. The audience gasped at the drama. That was exactly the desired reaction.

At intermission, it seemed he had done the impossible. The company hoped that now perhaps he would sit out the second half. His solos required a lot of energy, including speaking with the audience, and he had not been using a microphone lately. But he did them all, and wonderfully. And the entire second half of the show flowed as the first.

At the curtain call, he embraced Martha, as usual, except that day he cried.

After changing out of costume, Cesareo customarily walks to the lobby where he chats with company members. After cleaning and putting the show to bed, everyone stops to spend a few moments with him and say good-bye. That night he was sitting quietly in his chair, doing it all as usual. "He asked me to take his arm and help him to his chair," Igor said. "I felt honored."

Next Sunday he was "fine." Since his heart failure in 1993 and his pneumonia in 1998, "fine" might be qualified with a phrase something like this: performing on stage requires a "super" effort from him, and he gives it happily, week after week, year after year.

By the summer, Cesareo wanted to create a new opening to the show, "just to spice things up for everyone." On Saturday, September 10, he selected and recorded music for it. He chose a pulsing and richly melodic fandango for full orchestra with a brilliant brass section. The music is spine-tingling. He listened to it over and over sitting on a white couch by the grand piano at Avrom and Ann's house. Sometimes glancing out the glass sliders into the back yard and the forest that surrounds it, he noted who he had available then began to sketch a choreography. He listened to the orchestra with eyes closed, sometimes getting up to walk, as if measuring the steps from upstage to downstage in time with the fandango.

An hour later he leaned back, took off his glasses, and began to cry. "It is so beautiful, so absolutely beautiful," he said through his tears, as if it had come to him in a vision, whole and intact. He took a tape of the music to the theatre, where he played it for some of the company members, who were in tuxedo ready for the next film showing.

"Listen to it, get the music into your bones," he advised as they gathered about him at the concessions counter. He drew out their parts on a sheet of paper. "No more beginning in silence. This is a new era, a new world, a new season for our audiences. We begin with music now! We have only tomorrow morning to learn it," he said. Tomorrow would be Sunday, September 11, 2005. The season was to open in one week. He would have the stage in the morning until 1:30 when the movie matinee audience would enter. The next time the company would be able to rehearse with everyone there was Saturday, and Cesareo had other numbers to work on.

Sunday Cesareo began to work with pairs and small groups. A little after 10:00 he called everyone to sit in the front of the auditorium with him. "The music begins. Two curtains rise, one after the other, to reveal the tea house set with the golden stairs descending to the stage. On the upper level of the tea house, three enshrouded mysterious figures are frozen, bent over and somewhat concealed. The music continues. For the next twenty seconds only the empty stage with the three unmoving figures is visible to the audience.

"Then suddenly, all together, the rest of the cast bolts onto the stage from the wings like a sudden avalanche. This is a crashing wave, an eruption, a tremendous, overwhelming instant. From three stationary figures in the shadows to the entire company erupting onto the stage and then moving into a joyous fandango!"

He called everyone onto the stage. On either side of the golden stairs he marked seven positions with masking tape. He demonstrated the movements he was looking for as the cast moved from position to position, first by walking through it, then with the music, then with the two curtains rising with the music.

The timing needed improvement. Another run-through with the music. Why were the clowns approaching the stairs so late after the initial movements? That was corrected. Another run-through. We're ending too soon, there's too much music left. Instead of once around the positions, we'll go through them twice. Still not right. Cesareo comes onto the stage.

By now he is walking with a cane, speaking with more difficulty. It has been an hour and a half, and he has walked up and down from the stage a dozen times and more, and each time it requires more effort. It is clear that he is pushing himself beyond limits imposed by his health, trying everything to fulfill the dream, the vision he has so clearly seen for the new opening. It is as if he knows the finished piece is there, all the elements are there, and the company just has to jiggle and jostle things—themselves—to enable it to fall into place. So, he lines everyone up and says, follow me around the stage. "Music!"

He begins to dance the fandango and the company follows him, all thinking perhaps each in his own way, oh, so this is how it is. And dancing with him. And suddenly there is a new energy available to everyone, a new confidence.

OK, again, let's do it again. And this time the steps fill out the music and the timing is starting to work a little better. Cesareo: "We're going to go through the steps three times now, enlarge it, and we are going to stop here when Ellen and Perry are there." Everyone stops. He asks the dance captain to review it.

So the company walks through it, three times now, with stops arranged. Everyone stops when the two women reach the apex position on either side of the stairs. They are holding the banners and allow them to sway forward. In the middle of this explosive dance, suddenly everyone freezes and the only movements are these two women allowing their banners to sway gently toward the audience. Then bang! The dance begins again.

Now with the music, and it is starting to work. An adjustment here and there. Another repetition. By now it is noon, and Cesareo is two hours into the rehearsal. But this last time through seemed to work. The music ends. Cesareo walks up to the stage from his seat in the audience. He is crying. "This is how I envisioned it. Thank you. Thank you."

Everyone is buzzing on stage. There are many things to be checked and agreements to be made. And there is the good feeling of completion. One more time, Cesareo asks, or do we break for lunch? In unison, everyone says one more time. And again the timing is right, and it works. A happy ensemble puts things away, and prepares for what the afternoon may bring.

How quickly a medical emergency changes everything. With a month of successful performances of the new opening under the company's belt, three days after celebrating his seventy-third birthday onstage, Cesareo suffered a significant stroke in the early afternoon of Wednesday, October 19. The instantaneous response of his friend and former Salem State student Jerry, who owns a collectibles store a few doors up from the theatre, helped to speed the ambulance to the scene.

Jerry recalls: "That afternoon I was standing in front of my store when I saw Cesareo getting out of a car at the foot of the driveway to the parking lot behind the theatre. I turned my back for a moment, and when I turned around, I saw him leaning precipitously against a street post. Suddenly he toppled into the street. I knew it was serious and immediately called 911. Then I ran over to help."

David, who was a few steps ahead of Cesareo leading Blacky to the lobby, had heard a muffled sound, turned around and ran to Cesareo. He brought him into the office just a few steps away, bleeding where the pavement had gashed his forehead when he fell. Thanks to Jerry's immediate call, the EMTs arrived within minutes, staunched the bleeding and whisked him to Beverly Hospital where Dr. Ruff just happened to be on an unrelated matter. He received care immediately.

The stroke disabled his left side. He experienced pronounced weakness in the arm and leg on that side, and the left side of his face showed a slackening, slurring his speech. However his mental faculties were untouched, and he never lost consciousness throughout the entire event. From his gurney in the Emergency Room, as his street clothes were literally being cut off him, Cesareo commented that there was a show the next day. In fact the next evening, Thursday, October 20, the Larcom Theatre was scheduled to open with the autumn's premiere performance of *An Anthology of Stage Magic.*

After he'd been moved to a room in the Intensive Care Unit, Cesareo told David that he [Cesareo] could still perform in the show the next

212

night. Realizing that he had lost feeling and movement in his entire left side, he said, "I can get a cane or lean against a table." Having talked with Dr. Ruff, David knew there was no way Cesareo could be in the show, and he told Cesareo that he had better think about being in the hospital for a few more days. Cesareo conceded as much and went on to say that Rick, as his clown character Albert Ping-Pong, could fill in for his Larcom solo with a newspaper trick.

That evening the cast of the Larcom production gathered to work out all the substitutions and rehearse what was needed to perform the following night. David took charge of rehearsals. Off to one side of the auditorium, faithful Blacky lay quietly on the warm vest that had been cut from Cesareo earlier in the day.

As it turned out, the premiere the next night ran smoothly and was well received, bringing the audience to its feet at the finale. Having performed together for almost thirty years, the cast displayed a relaxed confidence and eye for improvisation that created the impression of a seamless show.

Katie played Cesareo's part in the Rabbit to Rooster production number. She handled the apparatus flawlessly, drawing the lanterns and silks out of nowhere with lilting movements, teasing winks, and disarming charm.

Cesareo asked Katie to perform two of his signature numbers for the upcoming Sunday show. "That Saturday evening I went to the hospital to visit Cesareo, clutching a bottle of cologne. When the girls were small children and they got a little boo boo or they fell down and scraped their knee, Cesareo would say, go get some perfume and put it on that spot, put it on the boo boo and that's going to make it OK.

We would sprinkle a little on, and they would run off and everything would be fine.

"As I peeked into his room, he was sitting there by himself, exercising his hands and wrists. I told him that everything was well set for the show, and told him that I brought him some perfume, reminding him of the story with the girls. I opened up the bottle and he put some on his forehead.

"We had a great conversation. There were just the two of us. I told him an idea I had for using a Carmen Miranda costume we had made for Martha many years ago. 'Katie,' he kidded me, 'you're taking over the show.' He was really encouraging. 'You can do this,' he said. 'Just have fun, be creative, have fun.' When I mentioned the fruit basket hat, he laughed and laughed.

"'Katie,' he said, 'you know what to do. When you're having fun, they're having fun.

"We talked about teaching the audience their trick. I asked him if he could remind me. So he went through it, saying you do this, and get them to do this, and they usually respond, and then we were talking about something else. I realized five minutes later, my gosh, I'm not going to remember that, so I asked Cesareo if he would go over it again, got my paper out and began taking notes. Lying there in bed, he was showing me with his hands how David exits from the Dancing Hank, and then he went through the sequence, telling me what he said to the audience. He told me what his internal dialogue is during that number, what he's thinking, how he's feeling. That was wonderful for me, and I think it was good for him, too, even in the midst of being all hooked up to oxygen in his nose and an intravenous line here and the tubes bringing medication there. Thinking of the show for him is like breathing in and breathing out."

Monday afternoon (October 24), Cesareo was transferred to Spaulding Rehabilitation Hospital in Boston. Up to this point, Dr. Ruff called his progress "almost miraculous." David stayed at Cesareo's side morning til night for his entire hospitalization (at moments Cesareo would be inclined to call it incarceration) at Spaulding. In addition to keeping Cesareo company, he learned the ins and outs of his medical treatments and physical therapy so that he could competently attend to Cesareo when he returned home. And that, for the stroke-sufferer struggling to right himself, could not be soon enough. Cesareo calls Spaulding "perhaps the finest in the country—they did a beautiful job with me."

Ever on guard for the well-being of his troupe, it occurred to Cesareo that the greatest way in which he could help the whole company while in the hospital was to send them reminders of the ideas and traditions that "we have made our own through the years." Every few days some of us would receive a page or two from a Maslow essay which Cesareo had asked Rick to reproduce for us. One of the recurrent themes was "transformation," the responsibility of a man to be open to the highest influences and to allow them to work their transformative wonders. Another was to live simply, honestly, and with gratitude. To watch Cesareo interact with the nurses and attendants in the hospital was heartwarming and inspirational. It seemed that no matter how much difficulty he was experiencing, he always strove to be attentive and caring toward the staff. He joked, complemented, and tried to make their time with him at least pleasant, if not uplifting.

Maslow had counselled that good psychological health meant being compassionate with yourself—forgiving, accepting of foibles and difficulties, and retaining the ability to smile and even have a good laugh about it all. There is always something restorative about being with Cesareo. His health-giving attitudes were especially evident now, and they were contagious.

He continued to make the day-to-day major decisions for the theatre from the hospital, and urged David, Rick and others to think from the heights. He suggested readings from some of Peter Brook's books, for example, "The theatre is perhaps one of the most difficult arts, for three connections must be accomplished simultaneously and in perfect harmony: links between the actor and his inner life, his partners and the audience," (*The Open Door*, by Peter Brook, 1993, p. 37).

Cesareo relied on readings in part because it was so difficult for him to talk due to the slackening of the muscles on the left side of his face. He received speech therapy to help him recover his ability to talk.

After his third week at Spaulding, he arranged for a day trip to Beverly. He attributed the success of the excursion to David's "temerity to sign and take me out on a Saturday from 9 a.m. to 6 p.m. They were giving me a necessary break." Cesareo wanted the simple pleasure of a shave (he had grown a beard) and a haircut at the barber shop a few doors from the Cabot. It was also the first time several members of the company had seen him since the stroke. His visit helped reduce their anxiety about him. It was a breath of fresh air not only for him, but for the whole company.

During this time he was pointing out what Maslow wrote at the end of his book, *Toward a Psychology of Being*. "It is not adaptation to disability that we must strive for in redefining health," Cesareo pointed out. "It's transcendence of disability." Together the company is learning about health as transcendence of environment.

Shortly after Cesareo left Spaulding as an in-patient, he learned about one of the world's leading authorities on stroke recovery whom Dr. Ruff had consulted from the outset. He is the head of his departments at Tufts University and St. Elizabeth's Hospital in Boston, and is also a magic aficionado. He had asked Dr. Ruff whether it might be possible to meet Cesareo. Following a dinner after a Sunday show in honor of Cesareo's doctors, he commented that the magic company's internal cohesiveness and cooperation, the working as an ensemble, are what he has wished for in his profession. "You do not insist on being recognized as individuals. So you have an effective ensemble."

Dr. Ruff said that he sometimes trembles in treating Cesareo, because he estimates he is treating a hundred people in the process. He realizes, conversely, that Cesareo has the support of a large group to help him recover.

Beginning at the holiday season, Cesareo went backstage with the cast during performances at the Cabot. He entered the stage only at the end of the curtain call. As soon as he came into the view, every audience spontaneously rose and gave him a thundering ovation. After one of those shows Ellen spoke for the entire company when she sent him this e-mail, "It was so wonderful to have you backstage again! Your presence certainly inspired the joyful spirit of the show from opening to finale."

217

Cesareo said, "the thoughts and talk over the months since this stroke led us to see clearly how much we love what we've put together, and how to use this opportunity to appreciate more deeply what we have."

On May 1, 2006, Cesareo wrote *MAGIC* magazine editor Shawn McMaster (as part of an interview conducted via e-mail):

> I am so happy today that it behooves me to share my joy with you. After spending the day at the Spaulding Rehabilitation Hospital in Boston, engaged in testing and reevaluation, the chief MD of physical medicine and rehabilitation released me from her care, which means she found me fine to keep on going in life. When I told the news to the cast members, they were all very happy; not to tell you that I was the happiest of all. I instantly began to say "thank you" to all members of the cast for their kindness and support over the last difficult months.
>
> And the biggest thanks of all and recognition was to David, Le Grand David himself, who steadfastly sustained the spirit of the show and kept the cherished dream of my entire life alive.
>
> Most importantly for me I have been permitted to take off my AFO (ankle/foot orthosis), so I can now easily wear all my regular costumes.
>
> Revealing the magic secret behind all this, for anyone who wishes to use it, is first to have a clear and definite aim; secondly imaginative visualizations, quietly seeing yourself in action as often as possible (called

directed dreaming in Jungian psychology); and thirdly to surround oneself with a cast of wonderful people who are constantly encouraging and positively supporting your efforts for recovery. Of course, take your medicine and rest and sleep well whenever time permits. In this case deep sleep is a great helper, and do your physical exercises, as recommended by your physical therapist, if possible twice a day. I've been doing them in the pool. Now I am even able to swim two lengths of the pool.

When he eventually returned to the stage, his chief doctor at Spaulding and practically the entire staff of nurses and therapists who had treated him attended a *Le Grand David* performance one Sunday. That comprehensive act of kindness and support left a generous impression in the collective memory of the magic company.

The company would observe first hand over the next year how attitude trumps neurology. One member of the company speaks for all when he said, "His stroke became, in a sense, ours. His regaining strength became ours. We joined the standing ovations he received as soon as he appeared on stage. When he returned to the stage that spring, barely six months after hospitalization, a large part of us returned to the stage with him." Much of what Cesareo lost to the stroke he gained back.

Marco's back, performing with a cane.

Le Grand David performing the Floating Ball.

Li'l Av - the artistry of clowning.

Le Grand David performing the Floating Ball.

Li'l Av clowning with the accordion.

Monkeying around in the Larcom show.

Katie clowning around on stage at the Larcom.

Katie dancing the rumba.

From left, Johnny Lapo, Katie, David and Ellen.

Queen Kathleen laughs
some every show.

Princess Perry spreads a
little sunshine.

Three *damiselas* in the Cabot finale.

Family portrait: Webster,
Katie, Marian and Martha.

Webster, Katie, Marian
and Martha.

Seth "the Sensational"
Always a Wonder to
Remember.

Hand-painted poster of
Marco and David.

Yankee Gathering
poster honoring
Ray and Ann Goulet.

John Fisher:
He is the very model of a
modern British gentleman.

Le Grand David:
the constant for
over thirty years.

Le Grand David bursts on
the scene.

Marco performs the Linking
Rings at the Larcom.

Marco with the Rings on
the Cabot stage.

Linking at the Larcom.

David and Marco pause
after a Cabot show.

Chapter Twenty: Sustaining and Enhancing

Compared to being exiled, this is nothing at all," Cesareo told a writer from the *Salem News*. "Do you know the Spanish word for exiled? *Destierro*. It means to be torn up by the roots. When you are exiled, you lose your language, your culture, your tradition. You have to start from zero. Compared with that, this [stroke] is nothing."

Around this time, David recorded Cesareo's advice to a young man who asked what was required to be a member of his magic company: "Devotion, sacrifice, endurance, effort, dedication, discipline, sensibility, inquisitiveness, and a constant quest for knowledge, love, thankfulness, respect for others and self-respect, genuine humbleness, and satisfaction when others succeed.

"But above all, give yourself fully to this art, which not only takes from us, but also provides our lives with incredible gifts."

On April 25, 2006, Cesareo returned to the stage. As the curtains rose that morning for *An Anthology of Stage Magic* at the Larcom Theatre, Cesareo entered the stage, opened his arms to the audience, and said boldly and clearly, "I'm back!" He received a joyous ovation in return.

He invited Henry Lewis to perform in this historic show. His good friend was now eighty-seven, suffering from a serious injury to his hand and mourning the recent loss of his wife of sixty years, Doris. "Yes," Henry said, "I am honored to come," and he arrived with props from his mentalism show. Matthew Field, editor of *The Magic Circular,* who saw Henry while he was preparing for this trip to Beverly, observed that he seemed in very good spirits, "considering the difficult year he has had. I am very glad he will be visiting with you and the Company—he loves all of you and I know the trip will be good for him."

Henry filled the twelve-minute solo slot that Cesareo usually performs towards the end of the show, allowing Cesareo a break near the finale. Cesareo told Shawn McMaster, "Our poster artist, Rick Heath, is painting beautiful canes for me to use in the show with Henry. Now I not only change costumes, but also canes . . . My aim now is to speak well, because good friends have told me that I've lost my accent since the stroke. So, I'm working to recover it before next Tuesday's show. Thankfully, Henry has a nice, deep British accent, and at his age I don't think he can lose it. We are like brothers, and I think we'll make a great team on stage. I'm sure the audience will know who is who by the accent.

"David is in charge of everything now, and he's even (protectively) bossing me around, reminding me of the things I need to remember to keep my progress on course. My doctor says that on paper I am healthy now. He's encouraging me to get back on stage."

After that inaugural performance, he told Shawn, "I knew fully at the end of the first twenty minutes that this was the most powerful moment of my life in thirty years on stage with this company: a single unrepeatable instant when our vision was transformed; the absolute sense of conviction that provided me with a glimpse of what we seek to achieve through the medium of stage magic."

Cesareo performed the first six numbers that open the Larcom show, each with its own scenery and music:

The Broom Suspension with David on Broom
The Animation and Vanish of Matter
Vanish and Reappearance of Human-Sized Rabbit
Truncated Parasol
Color Changing Plumes
Glass Portal Penetration

Cesareo has always been courageously direct and honest. Since the stroke, his sincerity has been overwhelming. It seems to be both more innocent and urgent—if that is possible—springing from a remarkable purity. Whomever he speaks with is bid by this circumstance to find his or her own deepest authenticity with which to respond. At company birthday parties and holiday dinners in the Grand Salon, you can bet that whoever sits with him for any length of time is coming from an honest and sincere place within.

This past Christmas (2006) in the Grand Salon, Cesareo was sitting with his good friend Ray Goulet. Later on Ray talked a little about his friendship with Cesareo. Ray was one of the first national magic figures to recognize this show as something extraordinary and a "must-see." When he first heard about *Le Grand David,* he figured it was a local show, nothing special. Then more and more people began to ask him if he had seen it. He began to make his own inquiries. He found out that it was still going on after four months, he decided to go.

He recalled:

> I was taken by everything. I asked people, where was it before it opened here? I went back to see it again. And again. I began to meet the people involved and I sensed a real closeness between them. They had a great feeling that was contagious. I kept getting a very friendly reception every time. Even after the show Cesareo made me feel welcome to stay and chat. It was unbelievable. That never happens.

> Cesareo and I hit it off from the beginning. He said to me, "I'm a trained doctor of psychology. You are a street doctor of psychology." That's because I can pretty much size up a person in a few minutes. I learned that from performing. You need to know who your audience is, especially if you are calling members of it onto the stage to assist you in some illusions.

> I'm as close to these people [looking around the room at the magic company] as if they were family. When he was thinking about buying the Larcom, Cesareo kept walking me down here. He asked me, "Would you be interested . . . ."

> Is this family? When you go for Christmas, New Years, Thanksgiving, and birthday parties every year, is this family? On these occasions, people around Boston no longer ask me what I'm doing. They ask, "Going to Beverly?"

> Cesareo is very up front. He can become irate, but it's

over in two minutes. He can go from one extreme to another, just like me.

One morning, before he went to the White House in 1985, I was sitting with him at the Cabot as he was rehearsing the company for the performance there. One woman was out of step each time. He was having the cast practice climbing the White House steps. "Do it again," he asked. Again she was out of step. She was the only one. And again. So finally he shouted at her, "You are not going to the White House!" He ran through it once more and she got it. From then on, she had it.

Cesareo said to me, Ray I want you to go come to the White House with us. So, I brought my favorite illusions from my childhood. Then in the middle of the performance it began to rain very hard, so we were taken inside the White House where we helped with the tours.

This trip to the White House is when I really began to feel we were part of one another. I taught Marian some tricks on that trip. She performed them for the company at parties. She was very proud of her tricks. Everyone in the company was happy to see her perform them. And I felt good about it because I knew that Cesareo would not let anyone else teach her.

You understand that for me friendship is very important. I have valued it more than anything since I was a young child because of the particular circumstances of my life. Make sure you note that, when this book is published, our friendship will still be going strong.

Cesareo keeps the membership in the company an educational experience. He keeps the people occupied with things that are important, rather than unimportant stuff. For example, all the men learn how to juggle as soon as they enter. They take piano lessons, learn carpentry, dance, music. Everyone who has passed through the company, and I have gotten to know practically all of them over thirty years, has accomplished something by being here, usually a great deal. The children make honor rolls. Even after they leave, they leave with a sense that they were meant to be successful, that life is there for living to the fullest and there is no other option. Everyone that enters these gates gets the sense that they are a winner in life. This is important stuff, not to be minimized.

After the Christmas meal began, Ray rose to make this toast: "To Cesareo, for bringing us all together. To you, the company, for allowing him to fulfill his dream. And to me, for becoming a part of this." From their seats, the company responded as one, "And to Ann [his wife, who had said grace] Viva Ann!"

After dinner Cesareo told the story of how he once saw a beautiful cabinet in Ray's museum and asked Ray to let him borrow it. "I'll paint it for you, it will look better on display," he said. "I brought it back, but after we painted it I liked it so much I decided to use it in our show."

Ray interjected that he didn't see the piece again. "I never said anything to Cesareo, but the next time I saw the Larcom show, there it was on stage, beautifully painted, as part of the Truncated Parasol illusion. He later gave me a replacement piece."

At the February 1, 2007, Larcom show the company had to respond to the last-minute unexpected absence of one of the members. Cesareo called Rick into his dressing room ten minutes before the opening curtain and arranged for the substitutions. He wrote Henry around midnight, after returning home from the performance, "It was a remarkable experience. Everyone pitched in, and from the audience perspective the show ran smoothly. At the end they were all on their feet applauding. When all is said and done, it was a very beautiful show. I performed the last forty-five minutes of the show without a cane [including the De Kolta Chair, during which he rushed upstage and pulled the drape off the chair to reveal that David has vanished]. These things can't be explained with ordinary language."

> The memories of the first years of my childhood are just being an audience for the little shows my older sister Elisa and her friends put on. They began to play at staging shows at the house. They put on Mother's shoes and hats, made themselves costumes, and sang and danced. They sat me in a chair to be their audience. I learned about theatre by watching it. About a year later, when I was four, my father began to take me to *Teatro la Caridad* to see shows.
>
> All of my closest friends loved theatre. I brought them together and we produced and performed shows at our

house for the neighborhood. We built the proscenium out of cardboard and papier maché, we constructed and painted our drops, sewed our curtains (with Aunt Aurora's help), built our own footlights, and sold tickets. We loved to joke around, we loved to sing and dance, we loved being with each other and we appreciated what we had.

My father loved the magic companies that came to town, like those of Fu Manchu and Chang. What extraordinary experiences . . .

. . .

Sometimes, now, when I awaken in the morning, I wonder how I would like to be within myself when I die. The answer is always the same: grateful. I would like to be thanking those highest powers that offered me this wonderful life.